TRUSTING A HIGHLANDER
THE SOULMATE CHRONICLES BOOK 1
Published by Keira Montclair
Copyright © 2017 by Keira Montclair

Cover Design and Interior Format

Trusting a HIGHLANDER

THE SOULMATE CHRONICLES ~ ONE

KEIRA MONTCLAIR

PROLOGUE

In the heavens, somewhere…

SHE HAD NO IDEA WHY she was here, this place of angels, of goodness, of the pure of heart. No part of that description applied to her last life at all.

Catherine followed the instructions of her guide, taking note of the number of people around her but not speaking to anyone.

"Your guiding angels will meet you in the Diamond Room." The woman pointed up a staircase, indicating the path she should take.

Catherine nodded to the woman and followed her directions. The staircase was wide enough to take up most of the foyer and it curved to the right at the top. The balustrade glittered with gemstones—diamonds, rubies, sapphires, and emeralds that beckoned the eye and begged to be touched—but when she reached out to brush one with her fingertips, they all blended together into a brilliant display.

Everything in the building was some shade of blue, her favorite color. The foyer was painted a teal blue, and as she climbed the staircase, she noticed the otherworldly ceiling. Sky blue with a domed window in the middle, fluffy clouds everywhere. Several doors were open on this level, revealing an array of different blues—a beautiful baby blue, a navy color, and a royal blue.

Heaven was almost exactly as she would have imagined.

She had no trouble finding her destination, the entrance open to all, so she ducked in through the threshold and located an enormous tufted chair at the back of the room. Sighing, she slid into it as quietly as possible. She wished she could recall all her previous lives, but the only life she could recall was the one she'd just left. It had been a hard-scrabble existence in the Americas in the year 1812. War and death begged to be erased from her mind, and the horrific memories continued to surface in her thoughts. She wished to have a more pleasant destination in her next life, whatever it would be.

She was exhausted. The end of her last life had been both draining and exhilarating. Humans were subjected to a "life in review" exercise at the end of each life cycle, or so the angel who led her through the experience had told her. This one had been as exhausting as her death. True, she had enjoyed seeing the highlights of her last life, the parts that had gone well, but the reminder of all her mistakes and errors in judgment had left her totally depleted and only interested in sleeping the day away.

If only she were allowed. How she wished she under-stood everything in the heavens, but the angels and other beings continued to be subtly secretive.

The room quickly filled with about forty people, a mix-ture of men and women, all dressed in modern clothes and quite beautiful for the most part. Her own clothes did not represent the life she'd just lived. The heels on her feet were definitely only from this world, and she wore a simple white blouse and a black pencil skirt. Many were dressed similarly.

As soon as the doors closed, a woman with dark skin and a bright smile glided to the front of the room and took her place behind a podium. Catherine took a deep breath, hoping for good news. She could certainly use an improvement over her last life cycle. Where would she go this time?

"Good afternoon and congratulations." The woman paused, taking a moment to look at each of them in turn. "My name is Evangeline, and I am here to tell you that you have each been promoted. You have exceeded God's expectations for you, so you will be given a new course for your next several lives.

"Before I describe your next few assignments to you, let me start by telling you that you are now a step away from becoming a guiding angel. You have each lived your lives upholding the moral code instilled in you, and you will be rewarded for your accomplishments."

Catherine enjoyed the swell of achievement blossoming inside her. She had finally done it! She would be moving ahead, and even though she didn't know exactly what it meant, it pleased her.

"But you have one last stage left to pass. You are to go through your next few life cycles with your soulmate. This person will travel with you to each life. Though you may not be together every day, you will spend more than half of your lives together. Your challenge in each life is the following: You must find your soulmate, you must reproduce, and you must teach the world something while you are there. It is our job to make the world a better place with each life, and that becomes even more important as you move ahead. Whatever you do, it must be something that affects many people."

The very word "soulmate" had snapped Catherine to attention. The concept of a soulmate was clear to her. You were from the same mold, so to speak. Soulmates believed in many of the same things, and they were drawn to each other inexplicably. Inevitably. Soulmates were always happier together than apart, and theirs was a bond that could not be broken.

Evangeline paused for a moment, then said, "That's it. You will be moved on to your next life within a few days. Questions?"

Several hands shot up. Evangeline nodded to the woman in the front row. "Yes?"

"How will we know where to find our soulmates?"

"Good question. Your soulmate is here now, and you will spend a couple of days together to ensure you are familiar with each other before you leave. We will make sure you meet in each life." She chuckled.

Catherine's gaze searched the room, and she noticed everyone else was doing the same, obviously hoping to find their soulmate in the room.

"Just meet?" someone else asked.

"Yes. You will meet, but it will never be easy for you. There will be several…challenges, shall we say? You must do whatever you can to battle through them in order to build a life together. That will be your focus. Of course, after you are reborn, you will no longer be consciously aware of your mission—or the identity of your soulmate. Your past lives are always hidden until you arrive back in heaven. Only by intuition and listening to your guiding and guardian angels will you know your path. As always, your success will depend on whether you will follow the angels' lead or fight them."

"Why is this a step up? This sounds more difficult than my last life." A thin man to Catherine's left posed this question.

"Another great question, and the answer is simple. The

best life on earth is the life of a person partnered with their soulmate. Once you connect with yours and meet your challenges, your existence will be, well, heavenly, if you'll pardon my pun."

Another hand raised hesitantly. "When do we meet our soulmates?"

"If there are no more questions, I'll send you off now to meet." She glanced around the room. "Oh, and you will have one guardian angel who travels with you through each life. You will meet various guiding angels, but your guardian angel will stay with you. One for you and one for your soulmate, though they may take different forms in each life."

She waited for any other questions, but there were none. It would seem Catherine wasn't the only one anxious to meet her soulmate. Butterflies had begun to burst to life in her belly.

"Off you go. Your soulmate is in this room, and you will have no trouble discovering which person is yours. You'll know as soon as you are close."

Catherine stepped away from her spot and started moving from chair to chair, already noticing a few couples hugging and greeting each other. She assessed each person she passed, but felt no special draw to any of them. She continued to walk until a warmth spread through her, beginning at her chest and spreading outward. He was near, she was sure. A few more steps brought her to a tall man with dark hair just long enough to hit his collar. He had blue eyes, eyes that reached down to her soul, a sure indication that he was her natural mate.

His gaze caught hers. "Is it you?" He reached for her hand, not to shake it, but to clasp it. His touch sizzled through her. "It must be you. I…I can feel your essence floating through me, almost as if you're branding me." His eyes lit up at the strange phenomenon.

"I feel it, too. It's as if you're moving through me, getting to know me, completing me." This last sensation was unlike any she'd ever experienced. "Yes, it's me. It must be."

After a moment, having found his answer, he pulled her close and wrapped his arms around her.

"This is where I belong, right here, with your arms around me. Do you feel the same way?" Her words came out in a husky, unfamiliar tone. She peeked up at him, wishing to memorize everything about this man. She wanted him in her life, in every life. It was just right.

Behind her, a voice carried through the haze surrounding the two of them. "Ah, Graeme and Catherine, you've found each other."

The angel clasped their shoulders and said, "You will be spectacular together."

CHAPTER ONE

The Highlands of Scotland, the 15th century

CATHERINE HATED HER HUSBAND.
    She sat in her chair—back rigid, hands folded in her lap just so—averting her eyes from the man bellowing in front of her.

"This is all your fault. If you were more of a woman, I would have no trouble performing, but you, you…"

Henry Merrill's face had turned an all-too-familiar shade of scarlet, making his brown eyes and brown hair darker in contrast. Though his features were handsome, he was too cold and cruel to be considered a good-looking man. What would her punishment be this time?

"Answer me. Why?"

"My lord, 'tis our daughter. I worry…"

His hand slammed down on the table, stopping her mid-sentence. "I do not care about her. Isbeil is female. And what are females worth, Catherine?"

She pinched her eyes shut, wishing such an act would make him disappear. She hated him more and more every day.

He loomed over her in the chair, pinching her chin to

raise her gaze to his. "What are females worth?"

She stared into his cruel brown eyes.

"Nothing," she whispered.

"You are worth nothing, as is our daughter. Nothing."

Even though her husband lived in Scotland, he'd been born an Englishman—and while he'd been banished to Scotland as a punishment, he still adhered to the ways of his former home. He never missed the chance to mock and belittle the Scots' speech and language, but her sire had sold her to the wealthy scoundrel as soon as he'd offered the right amount of coin.

"I have matters to attend to," the cruel man ground out, dropping his hand so he could return to his task of dressing. "It is your job to make me desire you, and you have failed again. You cannot even complete a task simple enough for a common whore. At this rate, I'll never get the heir that I need."

"Aye, my lord." She kept her gaze on her white hands, clasped together in her lap.

He sat in a chair and barked orders as he lifted his foot and pointed it in her direction. "Once you are finished dressing me, you will go to your spot in front of the hearth in the hall. You will kneel there until I tell you your punishment is over."

She rushed over to get his boot, which she helped pull over his swollen foot. Knowing she would pay for the next thing she would do, she moved ahead with her request as she laced the ties for him, unable to stop herself. "Isbeil is ill, and she is never let out of her room in the cellars. Please allow me to tend to her. I will complete my…"

His hand swung out, catching her square on her cheek with the back of it, the indentation of his ring scratching her tender skin. "I did not give you permission to speak. No, you shall not go to her. You'll do your punishment until I say you are done."

"Aye, my lord." She fought the tears that tried to escape, refusing to show him how he had hurt her. When she finished helping him dress, she followed him down the staircase and over to the hearth, keeping her head down so she would not have to see the looks everyone gave her. Some enjoyed the way he treated her; others felt sympathetic. Either way, it had happened enough times that she knew what to expect.

Catherine stood, as always, and waited for her husband to sift through the crate next to the hearth, searching for whatever form of torture he favored today. He pulled out one of the pieces that had been built according to his instructions. At least he'd chosen the device filled with pebbles. There were more painful options—a pouch he filled with fresh nettles before each use and another device studded with shards he'd collected from the armorer's hut. She prayed it would be kneeling today. Standing on the painful objects made it impossible for her to walk days afterward.

He sat in in front of her and said, "Kneel until I tell you that you are finished. Think about what you've done and mend your ways."

He always blamed her for his inability to maintain an erection after mauling her breasts and her tender skin. He barked orders at her, and she always did as she was told. How could she mend her ways? She had been upset about her daughter, so she'd offered distraction as an excuse, but mostly because she knew of no other. She did her best to stay groomed and clean. What more did he want from her?

In her darkest days, she admitted to herself that perhaps *this* was what he wanted. To see her suffer.

He shook his head, narrowing his gaze at her. "How

could I have ever thought you were worth the coin I paid for you? Aye, you are comely and shapely, but you have not given me the sons I require. Is that too much to ask from a wife? Bear me two sons, and I'll give you anything you want."

She knelt carefully, knowing from experience that how she landed on the pebbles would determine how painful her time would be.

"Enough. Kneel!"

She did as instructed and he stalked away from her, cursing as he moved.

In a small way, she was pleased.

No one would bother her, try to tell her what to do, or even speak to her during her punishment, which would give her plenty of time to think.

She needed to plan her escape. She would save her daughter, despite her husband.

Graeme MacGregor stood with his shoulders squared, his chin lifted to the late summer Highlands breeze, his favorite reminder of his sole purpose in life, to protect his lands. As laird of the MacGregor clan, it was his job to lead his clan, honor his ancestors, and fight for Scotland.

Honor his ancestors. That pledge alone forced one other duty upon his broad shoulders, but one he bore proudly.

Revenge. Revenge for the death of his parents and his eldest brother. Memories of the day he'd watched his family die at the hands of Henry Merrill would be ingrained in his mind forever. First his mother, then his eldest brother, then his sire. He'd watched, helpless, as his sire roared and fought, trying to rip free from his captors and save his wife…

And he had listened. He'd heard sounds and words he

wished to forget, words that had echoed in his mind every day since.

Henry Merrill would rue the day he'd made an enemy of Graeme MacGregor.

He took in the beauty of the majestic Highland peaks in front of him, letting the sight calm him. Those mountaintops reminded him of the vow he'd made on his sire's grave. His clan would be as glorious as that tallest peak. He was determined to see it happen.

He glanced over his shoulder when the rustling of his brothers reached his ear.

"Graeme, what's your decision?" Conn asked. Conn was two years behind him at nine and ten, and his youngest brother, Rory, was one and ten.

Graeme stared back at the peaks and breathed in the sweet morning air, listening, and finally he felt it. The serenity of the loch this morn and the slight breeze called to him, almost whispering his name in a soft chant. The peaks spoke to him as they often did. This day would be a special one. "We go today. The mountains tell me 'tis our time. Ready yourself and our men. We leave within the hour." The day was just breaking, and he preferred to travel in the early hours of the morn, just after the breaking of dawn. He heard the clap of hands at his declaration, and he knew it was his youngest brother Rory, anxious to move.

He and the MacGregor warriors would travel through the moors and valleys to Merrill land on a scouting mission to uncover more of the information they needed to attack the Merrills and kill their leader. He would strike down Merrill's clan just as Merrill had done to the MacGregors. Once they obtained all the information they needed from their scouting mission, he and his two brothers would plan their careful attack. Then Graeme would ready his two hundred Highland warriors, the force it had taken him years to rebuild and train, for the retaliation he'd vowed to take seven years ago. He'd been a lad of ten and four at the time, and it had taken patience for him to wait until they were ready.

That moment was finally upon them.

He turned to Conn and smiled. "This is to be our day."

His brother Rory asked, "How long have ye had these strange premonitions?"

He headed toward the stables to ready his horse. "Ever since the attack. You may trust that the mountains tell me this is a verra special day."

"In what way? We're not to attack the Merrills today—'tis just our last chance to gather information."

"Aye, and for Tomag to ready the men in the lists. We must practice hard and be ready. Dinnae worry yourself." Tomag was Graeme's second, and he'd assisted him in ensuring the men were trained for the coming fight.

He turned away from his brothers, waving at him to ready their small contingent while he completed a couple of final preparations of his own.

Before they left, he needed to visit their other brother.

Graeme went to see Boyd every day. The two of them had watched Merrill murder their parents and brother that fateful day. Conn and Rory had been inside the keep. The brutal attack in the courtyard had so traumatized Boyd, he'd stayed in his chamber ever since. Moyra, their head housekeeper, was his devoted caretaker.

Prior to this year, Boyd hadn't spoken a word to anyone after the attack, but he had finally emerged from his trauma enough to talk to one person: Graeme. Their conversations centered on one thing—killing the Merrill.

No one else knew about Boyd's progress. Graeme did not dare upset his brother, even by telling Conn and Rory.

The attack had traumatized all who'd witnessed it. Many of the MacGregor warriors had been killed, but some had been out hunting and had not returned until after the tragedy. Henry Merrill and his men had killed at will, cutting down all the warriors they could and slaying some of the clan who worked the land. Others had been left untouched. The only woman who'd been killed was Graeme's mother. Merrill had given no explanation for why he'd spared some and not others—except for Graeme. He'd made sure to tell Graeme why he was sparing *his* life.

He knocked on the door and stepped inside, knowing he would not get a response from Boyd. He found his brother pacing in front of the hearth in his room. "Boyd, is anything wrong?"

He stopped and spun around to face Graeme. "Today?"

Graeme nodded, taking in his brother's slight form, his pale skin. "Aye, today is our last scouting mission. We will finish this within a fortnight." He was so small for a lad of ten and four, but he never left the perceived safety of his chamber. Graeme had tried to convince him to go to the lists, practice working with a sword, but he'd refused. The lad who had once been fearless was now afraid of everything. That alone would have been reason enough for Graeme to seek revenge.

Boyd's eyes lit up and he asked, "Mayhap a sennight?"

"Probably a fortnight." Boyd's face fell, but Graeme knew how to hearten him. "It takes precision to do this right. If we dinnae, we could lose some of our men. Ye know we must be careful."

Boyd took a deep breath and smiled. "Be careful. I miss Mama and Papa."

"We all miss them. Are ye working on your letters? Ye know Mama wanted us all to read. She said 'twas important for the sons of the laird to be able to read the messages brought to them."

He nodded, holding up evidence of his work. "Rory and Moyra work with me every day."

"Good. That pleases me. I may need ye to assist me someday when ye are a bit older."

Boyd nodded, then whispered, "Go. 'Tis a most important day. I feel it, too. I knew ye would come to me with tidings."

Graeme pondered over his statement for just a moment before nodding in acceptance. Boyd knew things sometimes, there was no denying it.

Graeme had turned to leave when his brother stopped him again.

"Do not kill the wee ones."

Graeme jerked his head back to Boyd. "What? Ye do not wish to kill all the Merrills?"

Boyd shook his head.

"Our clan has demanded the blood of all the Merrill clan, women and children alike."

Boyd stared at his feet, his mind churning over something. Graeme could tell by the way he chewed the inside of his cheek that this was a difficult process for him. He'd often wondered what Boyd would have been like without the tragedy in their lives. Would he have been different anyway?

The lad lifted his gaze to Graeme and whispered, "I've learned 'tis wrong. The children have done nothing to us. We should allow them to live. Mayhap the women, too."

"You learned this? Where? How?" This went against everything his clan had demanded, everything he'd promised them. They wanted the Merrill clan to be put to death the same way Graeme's family and the MacGregor warriors had ruthlessly been cut down.

"In my sleep. It came to me then. I cannae explain, I just know 'twould be wrong. Kill the Merrill and his warriors. Leave the others."

Graeme did not know what to say to Boyd. While a small part of him agreed with his brother, he knew what his people wanted. How could he hope to sway them after seven years? "I cannae say ye are wrong. I'll think on it. 'Tis all I can promise, Boyd. Our men, our clan—they're hungry for justice. I must go now. The others are waiting."

"Godspeed. Protect Rory and Conn."

Graeme nodded and left the chamber.

He headed through the courtyard, his mind clouded by these new thoughts from Boyd. He knew not what to make of it. His brother had proven to know things, yet he did not understand how that could come to pass when he stayed in his chamber and spoke to no one other than Graeme. But his gut told him to trust Boyd's premonitions.

The decision did not need to be made this day, and he decided to put it off until after the scouting mission. He wanted—nay, demanded—precision for their final attack.

As soon as he arrived at the stables, the smell of horse calmed his blood. He took a deep breath and stepped inside.

The first rule for any great warrior was to care for your animal—in return, they would take care of you. Before they left, he would find a sweet treat for the beast and give him a thorough rub down, talk to him so he knew to be battle ready. He stopped at the treat barrel near the door, grabbing a few for his favorite beasts.

As he passed down the line of stalls, he stopped at his beloved mare's stall, put one end of a carrot between his teeth and held it for the bronze beauty. The horse greeted him with a nicker and trotted over to him, nuzzling his neck before she carefully bit down on the carrot and retreated, eager to finish her treat. Her antics made him chuckle. She was a fine animal, and with his stallion, she'd mothered two colts he adored. He called to her and she returned to his side so he could pat her neck before he headed down to the largest stall at the end, the one reserved for his pride and joy, Starlight.

He heard the swish of Starlight's tail before he entered his friend's stall. Starlight preened just a bit when Graeme entered, tossing his head with a whinny as a greeting to his handler. He pawed the ground with his front hoof as he often did in anticipation of his morning treat, a sweet apple that he preferred cut into two pieces. Graeme held the fruit and sliced it in half with his dirk before offering the first piece to the beast, who grabbed it and gobbled it down as if it was the most succulent meal ever. Starlight's bright eyes found Graeme's as he patiently awaited the second half. This one he chewed a bit slower while Graeme petted him and rubbed down his coat, talking sweetly to his horse as he always did to ready him for the challenging journey ahead.

He saddled the beast and brought him outside, taking another deep breath of the Highlands air to remind him of his purpose.

Once the others had all assembled outside, Conn asked, "Any special instructions?"

Before replying, Graeme surveyed his ten warriors— satisfied to see they appeared as ready for this mission as he was. "Nay. We proceed as planned. Conn, ye will take a contingency to the back of the castle to make sure ye know the landmarks and best places to climb the curtain wall, and Rory—" he nodded to his youngest brother, "— you and two men will continue to search for the hidden opening to the tunnel beneath the keep. We know there is a complicated maze there, and we must find it. I, along with Tomag and two others, will observe Merrill's schedule and try to determine the number of warriors he has at present. Any questions?"

No one replied, their serious expressions telling him his men wanted this almost as much as he did. "The reign of the Merrill will end in less than a fortnight. We make our final plans after this excursion."

His warriors responded the same as they always did, chants of "MacGregor, MacGregor" filling the area. The loud, booming voices of his men drew other people out of their homes, and their voices joined in with mantras of their own.

"Kill the Merrills, kill the Merrills!" Their voices rose and the excitement of the crowd peaked. "Kill them all. Time to die!"

The chants were usually the same. Something niggled at the back of his mind—Boyd's words. Conn had told him the same thing many times. *Kill only the warriors. They are the ones who killed our family, our clan.*

Graeme led the others down the path that ran between their cottages, listening to the fervor of their voices. The warriors who had missed the tragedy because they'd been hunting had been overcome with guilt over the event. They wanted all the Merrills dead. He had felt the same way after witnessing the horrors of that day, but something now told him it was wrong. He couldn't say what—no different than Boyd. Had he and his brother shared the same dream? Something told him to spare the women, the children, the elderly. Would the people truly accept such a command from their laird?

He could not guess. The entire experience had been traumatic. Some cottages had been burned to the ground. The clanmates who'd survived had rebuilt their huts, but rebuilding his group of warriors had been more difficult. Some families had left the clan, fearing they'd face another attack with few warriors left to defend them.

But he *had* rebuilt. Their numbers were high again, and he was confident the MacGregors would prevail over the Merrills. It had been a long, arduous journey for them, but he had to believe they would become a prosperous clan again.

As they moved through the outer bailey, the few lasses who had stayed with his clan came out, casting coy looks his way. He knew what they wanted—*him.*

Graeme had not had time to focus on a woman. He was single-minded in his goal to regain the power his clan had possessed before the attack—to make the Merrill pay for what he'd done. He had no time to wed or court a lass, though many said his clan needed a mistress. Someday he would find a woman who interested him enough to court her, but not yet.

As Graeme and his lads made their way to the end of the path, he let out the MacGregor war whoop and spurred his horse into a gallop. They could be as loud as they wished while still on MacGregor land, but once they crossed into Merrill land, his men would turn silent. The beast responded with a snort and a charge that made Graeme grin. Even Starlight was eager for their mission.

CHAPTER TWO

CATHERINE SAT IN HER CHAMBER near the fire. Her maid, Dolag, had wrapped her bloodied knees in linens after applying a soothing ointment, but they still pained her. After Catherine had passed out from the pain of kneeling and the lack of water, her manservant, Benneit, had carried her up to the room. He was one of her rare allies in the castle. The door opened and Henry's sister, Margaret, swept inside. She had become another, unexpected, ally. However, as much as Catherine hated her husband, she trusted Margaret completely. She had proven repeatedly that her love for Isbeil was true, and this meant more to Catherine than anything else she could do.

"My dear, Catherine. What has my foolish brother done to you this time? And why did he insist on another punishment?" She clucked her tongue as her hands settled on her slim hips. Margaret was an attractive woman with smooth dark hair and warm brown eyes.

"The same reason, Margaret. Do not concern yourself. Until I give him the son he wishes for so desperately, he'll not leave me be." She swiped at her eyes, refusing to give in to her tears.

"I wish there was a magic potion to get a woman with

a male child. How many women find themselves in this very position?" Margaret's husband had died from a sword wound, but he'd begged her for a son often before she'd finally had Wesley. It had soured their marriage. "Foolishness. Just foolishness that they believe we have any control over what kind of child we carry in our womb. I would like to take up spells and incantations, see if it does any better than leaving it to nature."

"How is sweet Wes?" Catherine adored her dear nephew almost as much as Isbeil. Wesley was two years older than Issy, and he was the only child Issy was allowed to see. Henry and his mother had tried to forbid it, though Catherine never understood why, but Margaret ignored them both. What would she do without Margaret? She was her only true friend other than her dear servants.

"Wes is a bit sickly, so I've left him abed. I will not bring him to visit Issy today. Are you going down to see her?"

"Aye, Henry gave me permission for a short visit."

"Allow me to help you. I'll assist you down the stairs into the cellars."

Catherine said, "Many thanks to ye. I did not know if I could make it on my own."

"Ah, but I know you well, dear sister. You would find a way. Ready?" Margaret asked.

Catherine nodded and hoisted herself to a standing position. She stood in one place for a few moments to adjust herself to the pain in her knees.

Margaret shook her head as she watched Catherine. "How you bear so much pain, I'll never understand. My brother is a lout, and I tell him so every time I see him." She looped her arm through Catherine's and encouraged her to lean against her.

Catherine let out a slow breath and stepped forward, steeling herself not to cry out. "I can do this. If ye help me down the stairs, I'll be able to manage the rest of the distance."

It was a slow trip, but Margaret managed to get her to the cellars without Catherine crying out once, a wonderful accomplishment. Margaret bussed her cheek and said, "There you be. Now go enjoy your beautiful daughter and please give her a kiss for me."

Catherine hobbled down the dark passageway as best she could just as Benneit caught up with her. She would do all she could to hide her pain from her sweet daughter—the sole light in her life.

What Henry did not realize is that she would gladly go through worse in order to hold Issy in her arms again. She stood back and allowed Benneit to open the heavy wooden door guarded by two of her husband's strongest men. They stared over her shoulder, ignoring her as they oft did. Henry did not allow his men to speak to her, only Benneit. Grateful for Benneit's assistance, she smiled at him before stepping inside the dank chamber in the basement of the castle.

Once inside, she shivered at the chill in the air. How she hated that Henry had banished Isbeil to the cold, damp cellars. She was the laird's daughter and deserved better quarters, but he refused to give in to Catherine's request to keep her daughter with her. She believed the tiny chamber was partly to blame for Isbeil's poor condition, but no one would listen to her, and her husband, frankly, did not care. The sight of his small daughter only seemed to remind him that he did not yet have the son he wanted.

"Greetings, Lady Rodina." She hated addressing her husband's mother in such a way, but she would do whatever necessary to see her daughter. "How does Isbeil fare?"

Her daughter's head turned on the pillow toward her. "Mama!" She held her thin arms up to her mother.

Rodina pushed her heavy frame off the cushioned chair she sat upon and moved to the opposite side of the sparse chamber. A basket of food sat atop the small table, and she popped a pastry into her mouth. Catherine knew better than to ask whether Isbeil had been given a pastry or a piece of fruit. Rodina had determined that the lass needed nothing more than porridge and stale bread. It was a true testament to her daughter's sweet nature that she never complained.

Rodina brushed the thin gray strands back from her face and chewed the treat before she spoke. "More sickly every day. I have told my son that it is your bad blood that causes her sickness. I hope he never gets you with child again. You're a terrible mother."

Catherine ignored her rude comments, so accustomed to them that she never listened anymore. It was a true wonder how Margaret had come from such a woman. She sat on the bed and tugged her tiny daughter onto her lap, wrapping her arms around the wee thing and inhaling her sweet scent.

"Mama, why do ye walk funny?"

"Oh, I fell outside on the stones. Do not concern yourself. Now tell me about how my dear Issy fares."

"I looked at the picture book ye brought me. I've read it three times."

Catherine chuckled because she knew her daughter could not read at four summers—though someday she hoped to teach her—but what harm could it do to allow her to believe it? "Three times? It must be a special book indeed. Why do ye not tell me all about it?"

Issy replied, "I love this book about the beautiful deer and the puppies. 'Tis a most wondrous thing. Do ye believe I could have a puppy someday?"

Catherine held her daughter's face between her palms,

cupping her sweet cheeks, thinner than they should be. "Ye never know what may happen someday."

Rodina barked, "No, there'll be no filthy dogs in here with her. I'd never allow it."

"Please, Mama?" Issy's warm breath tickled her ear.

Catherine whispered back, "We'll see, my dear. There's always hope for a better day."

Rodina guffawed. "You are a fool if you believe anything she tells you, girl."

Issy chattered away until fatigue overtook her. "Mama, I do not feel well," she said in a small voice, leaning her head on her mother's shoulders.

Catherine fought tears. "I'm so sorry, wee one. How I wish I could stop your illness, give ye some motivation to dance on the floor."

"Mama, I'm so tired. I must close my eyes. Will ye hold me?"

"Of course."

She loved it when her daughter fell asleep in her lap. Issy's sweet aroma drifted up to her, and she rested her chin on her daughter's hair, red just like hers. The lassie was so sickly—and had been for a year. There was only one thing she could do to help her.

After much consternation, she'd come up with a plan. She'd escape and travel back to her parents' home to seek out the old healer there. She could not recall the woman's name, but her mother had told her she had mysterious and gifted hands, sometimes able to drive sickness away when no one else could.

The Merrills had no healer, so poor Issy suffered. Catherine had begged Henry to send for one, just for the wee lass, but he had refused. Though she knew the price she was likely to pay for seeking out a healer's knowledge in defiance of her husband's commands, she could not stand by and watch her only daughter die a slow death.

Aye. The time had come.

Catherine was not without allies, and Benneit had vowed to help her sneak outside this night. Then she would travel to her mother's healer and, hopefully, learn how to cure her daughter.

Her husband was away, so it was the perfect opportunity. True, she would struggle with the pain in her knees, but after spending most of the day healing, she would be able to manage. She had to. Henry was not gone often. Without a doubt, her pain would ease as soon as she mounted her horse.

She would find help for her daughter, even if her life was forfeit.

Later that night, Benneit knocked on the door of Catherine's private chamber, the place she slept until her husband beckoned her to his chamber. She bade him to enter, and he did so, closing the door silently behind him.

Benneit whispered, "Here, my lady. Don these things. 'Tis three hours past midnight, so ye should be safe to leave at this hour. You will look like a lad with your hair under the hood, which should get ye by the guards at the gate. I shall walk with ye to guarantee your safety, but only until the end of our land. Then I will part from ye."

"Benneit, ye need not travel so far with us. If you are caught, he will kill ye for certain."

"I know, but I cannot allow ye to travel alone in good conscience. But I must return, or they will send someone after me. You understand?"

"Aye. I will make it. I promise you."

"How are your knees? 'Tis too soon for ye to be walking."

She pressed against the bandages and winced just a bit. "They have improved much with the poultice. I cannae wait until they heal. Ye know my husband is rarely gone. I will do fine on the horse."

"There is a dirk hidden in the jacket. Use it if ye must."

Once she had donned the outfit, they crept down the staircase and across the courtyard to the stables. He waved to the guards at the gate, though two of them appeared to be sleeping. With the lord gone, they were lax in their duties.

Catherine breathed a sigh of relief when they were out of view of the castle. She slowed her horse to speak to her friend. "We did it, Benneit. I will forever be grateful to you."

"Nay, my lady. 'Tis my duty to care for ye. Keep your hood up and travel in that direction." He reminded her of the landmarks she needed to look for in order to get back to her land, though she would not make it until the morrow. Her hands shook at the realization that she was free of her husband, if only for a short time. Once she neared her sire's lands, she would have to tread carefully. He would be almost as furious as her husband if he discovered she'd left her keep without permission. "Please be careful with the horse. He is not the strongest, so 'twill take a few hours to get to MacGregor land. Try to travel on the edge of their land as much as possible. Ye dinnae wish to be caught as a woman traveling alone, especially not there. They've no fondness for the Merrills."

If not for Issy, she would keep riding forever and never return. She said goodbye to her friend and flicked the reins of her horse. The last thing she heard was Benneit saying, "Godspeed, my lady."

She traveled without stopping until shortly after dawn, but her bladder could not tolerate the bounce of the horse any longer, so she was forced to stop. She found a small clearing in the forest and dismounted, stopping to listen first for any activity. Confident that she was alone, she moved over behind a bush and relieved herself. As soon as she had her trews belted again, she found her way back to her horse, only to hear a snort behind her.

Turning around slowly, her heart sped up at the sight in front of her—a wild boar that had just noticed her. She screamed and ran for her horse, but her mount had caught sight of the beast, too. To her horror, he galloped away in the opposite direction.

Her gaze scanned the area for a tree she could climb, and she raced toward one with low branches, her heart now in her throat as fear hurtled through her veins. She jumped for the lowest branch of the tree and grabbed it as the boar charged toward her. Hanging from the branch, she curled her feet up to her waist, praying she was high enough to escape its attack. Its jaw clamped onto the boot of her left foot, and she lost her grip on the tree branch and tumbled down to the ground. Her foot now free, she kicked the beast and scrambled backward, ignoring the pain shooting up her leg and grabbing for the dirk in her pocket. She managed to stab it three times before its snout shoved at her, pushing her down an embankment.

The boar squealed from its wounds, running in a circle before it slowed, turned toward her once again, and charged directly at her, following her down the hillock. She managed to stand up, but there was no time to run. All she could do was flail her weapon at the animal. She stayed on her feet and screamed as the beast's ugly jaws opened to bite her.

She was a dead woman. What would happen to Issy?

They'd almost reached Merrill land when an eerie premonition permeated Graeme's body, a feeling deep in his gut he could not ignore. He slowed his horse, allowing the others to ride ahead of him.

"What is it?" Conn asked.

A blood-curdling scream echoed through the trees. "That," Graeme replied. "You wait here with the men. I'll see what it is."

"You're the laird. Ye should send us ahead of you. How many times must I tell ye that? 'Twas always our sire's rule." Conn glared at his brother.

Rory came abreast of them. "I'll go, Graeme. Allow me, please?"

"Nay." He turned his horse toward the sound. "My gut says I go alone. Wait here."

Graeme led his horse through the forest toward the sound. He was sure it was a woman, but what would a woman be doing in the middle of the forest? A short distance later, he came upon the source of the scream.

A lad—nay, he realized, a lass *dressed* as a lad—had fallen down an embankment, and a wild boar was headed straight for her. She screamed again as the beast bore down on her, hitting her with its snout and sending her reeling backward. Somehow she managed to stay on her feet, slashing at the animal with a dirk, connecting with its flesh enough to enrage it more.

Spurring his horse, Graeme rode straight for her and then leaned over and scooped her up just as the boar's jaw opened in anticipation of a sweet meal.

She landed on his lap with a grunt, clinging to him as if he'd saved her life, which he supposed he had. If not, he'd definitely saved her from a painful attack. He rode back toward his men, the boar in pursuit for a short distance before it gave up to lick its wounds, squealing and snorting its anger first.

The lass sat facing him in the saddle, and once it was clear they were safe, she pulled her head back and stared up at him, her mouth forming a perfect circle.

Graeme sucked in a breath. She was a beauty unlike any other. Green eyes the color of the forest stared at him, fringed with long lashes. Her high cheekbones were gloriously flushed, a color that matched her lips. He wished to see what color her hair was under the hood.

"Who are you?" she asked. "Leave me be, I'll find my horse. Many thanks for saving me, but I must be on my way." She spoke in a clearly disguised voice, attempting to act the boy in her lad's costume. This woman would never deceive anyone who came close enough to see her delicate face.

"Are ye alone, lad?" Graeme did his best to hide his smirk, playing along with her ruse.

"Aye. Please release me. I must continue my journey."

He tugged on her hood and a long plait of glorious red hair fell down her back. She glowered at him and said, "Stop."

He stopped his horse and quirked his brow at her, a slow grin crossing his face. "Aye, *lad*?"

Her gaze narrowed and she glowered at him. "Fine. I'm no' a lad."

"Aye, 'tis true. I knew that even before your curves landed in my arms. Where are ye traveling on your own? A lass cannae travel alone in the Highlands. Or mayhap ye are lost from your party?"

"I'm in desperate need of a healer. Please allow me to continue on my journey."

"Your name?" He brushed several loose hairs out of her eyes.

"Catherine. 'Tis all ye need to know. Leave me be. I

must find a healer."

Catherine. The sound of her name sent a chill down his spine. He had the strangest feeling that he knew her, but they'd certainly never met. The notion was completely preposterous, so he chose to ignore it. "For your own wounds or those of another?"

Clearly incensed, she swung at him and hit him in the arm. He'd watched the feisty lass stab a wild boar several times. Would she do the same to him? She hit him again, harder this time, though it felt like little more than a tap.

The last thing he needed was for his plan to be delayed because a lass had stabbed him. He had to head to Merrill land, finish the plan he'd formulated for years. Graeme believed in following his gut, and his gut had told him it was to be an important day. Such a message was not to be ignored.

"As you wish," he said. He lifted the lass off his horse and set her on the ground. She promptly collapsed, grabbing at her foot. Though impatient to turn back toward his men, he found himself watching her as she attempted to limp away.

His sire's voice echoed through his mind: "A man is honor bound to protect a lass in need." It was something he'd taught all five of his lads over and over again. A Highlander's honor meant he must always assist woman and children, protect them when necessary. The beautiful Catherine, hurt by a boar and without any horse that he had seen, most definitely qualified as a lass in need.

He could not leave her.

Cursing, he dismounted and hurried over to her. Before he reached her, she fell to a heap on the ground again. It was then he noticed the blood on her legs and feet. He couldn't leave her alone like this. His honor as a Highlander demanded it. He knelt down next to her and scooped her up into his arms.

She swung at him, her arms flailing, tears pouring down her face. "Nay, nay, please. I must save Issy." She fought kicking and screaming, but he wouldn't let her go.

He didn't understand why she fought him so. It would be madness to leave her here, in the middle of nowhere, with no horse in sight. Besides, for some strange reason, he believed she belonged in his arms.

CHAPTER THREE

T HIS ISSY HAD TO BE someone special if she was the reason for Catherine's journey through the woods.

"Hush, wee Catherine," he said softly. He understood what it was to feel unbridled fear and confusion. He'd been in the exact same place seven years ago. She needed soothing to settle. "Where is your horse?"

A lone tear slid down her cheek and her chin quivered. Her forest green eyes were veiled in a mist that he wished to drive away. "He ran when the boar charged. I must find him before they find me."

"Who?" He bristled at the thought of anyone chasing her, intending her harm. "Who is after you?"

"My husband's guards. They could find me. Please. I must be on my way. Lend me your horse, and I'll return it soon. I promise."

A small smile crept across his face. The lass was truly an innocent if she thought she could traverse the Highlands alone and return unharmed.

"Who is your husband?"

"Ye dinnae need to know."

"Keep your secrets for now, but I cannae allow ye to go on this journey ye have planned for yourself. 'Tis too dan-

gerous. You'll travel with me to my land, and I'll see your
wounds cared for, then we'll discuss how I can assist ye.
Have ye not noticed the state of your legs and feet? You'll
be in agony when ye do." The lass was obviously in shock
after the boar's attack.

She set her hand on her left foot and then turned her
fingers around to view the blood now dripping down her
hand. "My foot," she said in surprise. "I cannae move it."

He set her down on the ground. "We must remove your
boot now, before it swells. Give me your ankle." He held
his hand out to her.

Her gaze lifted to his and he almost lost his balance. The
power of her gaze was like nothing he'd ever experienced.
Though he knew so little about this woman, there was no
denying there was a connection between them. Damn,
but what power did she hold over him?

After a pause, she lifted her boot up to his hand, winc-
ing at the pain. "Your name? Ye have not told me. I'll not
allow a man to touch my skin if I dinnae know his name."
She blushed and stared at her mangled boot.

"Graeme. Graeme MacGregor."

Her eyes widened. "The laird of the MacGregor clan?"

"Aye. Now do ye trust me not to hurt ye without due
cause?"

She nodded with a quick glance and a blush. "Please be
careful."

Catherine could feel the heat of his gaze—Graeme
MacGregor, the renowned laird of the MacGregor clan.
She'd heard he was a cold-hearted bastard, driven by some
tragedy in his clan's past. She'd heard whispers about a
massacre at the MacGregors, but she'd been young at the
time—it had happened the year before her sire sold her to

the Merrill at the tender age of ten and seven. Her sire had always believed in keeping the women of his clan ignorant of the goings-on in the Highlands, and her husband was no different. There was gossip at the Merrill's keep, but none of the servants other than her friends included her in their talk.

Whatever the gossips said, this man was far from cold-hearted. He removed her boot with surprising gentleness.

His voice low, he whispered, "Tell me if I'm hurting ye." He removed her woolen stocking and assessed the damage done by the teeth of the boar. "I'll bind it and treat it with a poultice when we get to my castle." He used his dirk to cut a long strip from his plaid.

Catherine peeked up at him. The man was beyond handsome and exuded raw, masculine power. His strong chiseled jaw bore a touch of stubble, and his kind smile had revealed the whitest of teeth. Graeme's hair, almost black, fell past his shoulders, and it shamed her how much she wished to run her fingers down the length of the strands. When he lifted his gaze to hers, she felt as if his blue eyes reached in and touched her soul.

There could not be a single man in Scotland more different from her husband.

When he finished tying the strip around her foot to stem the bleeding, he said, "Grab my arm and I'll help ye to stand. We'll see if ye can walk on it. If not, I'll carry you." He shoved what was left of her boot into his saddle bag.

She nodded, unable to speak with him so close. He discomfited her in a way she did not understand, and yet he also made her feel strangely…at home. She gripped his upper arm, surprised at the size of it, and found she needed to use both hands on his bicep to manage her weight. Her right foot, still booted, held her weight, but it was bleeding from wounds of its own. Catherine was not in good shape, and somehow she knew she would not be continuing her journey for a day or two. Unable to walk without pain shooting through her body, she leaned toward Graeme, who promptly scooped her back up.

Never had she met a man as large as Graeme MacGregor.

Or as tender.

After Graeme set Catherine atop his horse, he mounted behind her and flicked the reins, heading back toward the path. His warriors awaited him not far from the point where he'd left them.

"'Tis a lad or a lady, Graeme?" Rory asked.

Conn stared at Graeme, a surprised look on his face. None of his men spoke, but every gaze was on the beautiful lass in front of him. It was obvious they had all guessed the answer to Rory's question.

"Catherine was wounded by a boar, and her wounds need tending. I will take her back to the keep. Continue the plan we had in place. You all know what to do. You do not need me along."

Conn's gaze widened. "She traveled alone?"

Graeme nodded.

His second, Tomag, asked, "Where is she from? Mayhap she is interested in joining our clan."

Graeme clenched his teeth and ground out, "She's mine. Take your gaze from her, all of you. You'll not touch her. Be on your way and report back to me as soon as possible." He hadn't intended to speak so harshly, but while Tomag's question was innocent, Graeme felt the need to declare that she was off limits to all.

A strong voice surprised him. "I'm no' yours."

"Aye, my laird." Tomag bowed his head, his way of apologizing for overstepping his bounds, but Graeme could not blame him. Tomag had been a faithful second to his sire for years, so he held a great deal of respect for the man. He trusted him completely.

Then why had he felt compelled to speak to him so sharply about Catherine?

The MacGregor men had not seen a lass this comely in a long time. Graeme turned his horse around and whispered into Catherine's ear, "Aye, ye are for now, lass. Ye do not wish to be available to anyone but me. My men have not seen many women in a long time."

"I'm married. Do no' forget it, if ye please."

Graeme hid his shock at her statement, but then he recalled she'd mentioned her husband's guards. Apparently, he'd chosen to ignore what that meant. But what man would allow his wife to travel alone in the Highlands? Something was not right, and he would find out. If she was running away, he wished to know her reasons. He tugged her closer on his horse and said, "Trust me, I willnae forget."

They were not far from his keep, but she quickly fell asleep in front of him, leaning back into his chest. He found he quite liked her there, her presence inciting a feeling of protectiveness he could not deny. Once he slowed his horse and approached the gate, the yelling from his guards on the curtain wall awakened her.

"Laird, where are the other men?" one of the lads asked.

"They are finishing their task. Dinnae worry about them." They opened the gates, and Graeme rode over the bridge and moved through the cottages in his inner bailey. Men came out to gaze at his companion, but he made it clear with his carefully placed glower that Catherine was unavailable to anyone.

"Where are the women of your clan?" she whispered.

"We have some left. Most have sought other clans, though I know not why. We lost many warriors after an attack on my clan, and others left for fear of another incident. We've worked hard to rebuild. My men work hard to train for our ultimate battle. Perhaps they did not have enough time to suit the lasses." When they reached the stairs to his keep, he stopped his horse and threw the reins to one of the stable lads that had followed him. As soon as he dismounted, he reached up to put his hands on her waist, but she flinched.

He stood back and placed his hands on his hips. Why would the lass flinch from his touch? He had an inkling he did not like. A small crowd had gathered, watching the two of them, curiosity overtaking their better sense. "Go back to your work and dinnae concern yourself with the lass. She is my concern only," he barked, making sure they scurried away before he glanced back up at her. He had to admire a lass who sat so straight, so proud under the scrutiny of so many strangers.

When she dropped her gaze to his, he said, "Do ye not trust me? Do ye believe I will hurt you?"

She shook her head, her eyes misting again. "I trust ye, I just…my legs pain me terribly."

He reached for her again, and this time she did not shrink from his touch. As soon as he had her on the ground, he scooped her into his arms so he could carry her up the stairs and into the MacGregor great hall. "Moyra!" he shouted as he strode inside. He found a table and set Catherine atop it so she could support her leg on the bench, allowing him to see her wounds better.

In a matter of minutes, an older woman bustled out of a door at the far end of the hall. "Aye, my laird? Ye are back so soon."

Moyra stopped in her tracks when her gaze fell on the slight form atop the table. "My laird?" She stopped when she reached them, awaiting his instructions.

"Moyra, this is Lady Catherine. I came upon her when she was being attacked by a boar. She has a few wounds that need tending. Please take her to my chamber and tend them. I will be back after I check in with my men. Before I leave, I'll send a couple of lads in to carry the tub into my chamber and assist with hot water. She is not to leave my chamber until I return."

He nodded and then turned his back to them, but he'd only taken two steps toward the door when a voice stopped him in his tracks.

"How dare you! Ye have no ownership over me. I will gladly accept Moyra's help with my wounds, but I'll not stay here a moment longer than need be. As soon as I am able, I will leave on my own accord. I willnae wait for your permission."

Graeme hid his smirk. Damn, but she was a feisty one—as fiery as her red hair. He turned around in a slow circle until he met her gaze. Then he strolled back across the hall toward her, the expression on his face enough to make Moyra take a few steps back.

When he stopped in front of her, he lifted her chin to force her gaze to his, but she swiped at his hand and pulled back. "Do no' touch me."

This time he did not hide his smirk. "No appreciation for saving ye from the jaws of the wild boar, my lady?"

"I do appreciate your assistance, but I'll not be run by you. There are enough men in my life who tell me what to do and when to do it. I'll not stand for another stepping in to take over."

Graeme felt something he hadn't felt in quite a while. His erection had popped up so fast, it shocked him. The woman was as enticing as they came. The fury in her eyes could match his own when someone riled him. Damn, but he wished to have this woman under him, writhing beneath him as she screamed his name while he pleasured her.

He reminded himself that he lusted for a married woman. That would not do, though he would not rest until he discovered who her husband was and why he'd allowed her to travel alone.

He whispered, "When ye are in my keep, you'll do as I say. I will respect that ye are a married woman, but you'll not chase around as ye wish. 'Tis my duty to protect ye, and allowing you to prance around in front of my men is asking for trouble. If I must lock the door, I will. Do we understand each other?" He brushed his thumb across her cheek, and he was surprised that she allowed it.

"Aye, Laird MacGregor."

If the expression on her face was any indication, he would have an interesting time with Lady Catherine, whomever she was.

CHAPTER FOUR

I F CATHERINE DARED, SHE WOULD have slapped him for saying that.

But the way he'd touched her… She'd never been touched by any man that way before, which was the only reason she'd allowed the soft caress. Her husband had certainly never touched her with gentleness. This man was a complete mystery. Demanding yet tender. Moody yet kind. She wished to yell at him more, but he was quite a bit larger than she was, and the pain grew with every passing moment. For now, it would be better to allow him to think she would do as he said.

Which she wouldn't. Isbeil was foremost in her mind. She would allow Moyra to help her and then ask if the woman had any suggestions about Isbeil's condition. The fact that the laird was taking his leave was perfect.

"Come, my lady," Moyra said. "I'll assist ye into his chamber up the stairs and at the end of the hall."

Catherine smiled at the older woman. Her hair had been dark at one point but was now peppered with gray. She had bright eyes and a kind smile. Catherine noticed the calluses on the woman's hands, evidence of how hard she worked. With any luck, she would be a great source of information.

She followed her into the laird's chamber just as two lads carried a tub into the chamber and then quickly left. She'd never seen anyone move that quickly for her husband. Glancing at the walls of his chamber, Catherine saw nothing pleasing to the eye, only various weapons. Otherwise, the chamber was cold and stark, furnished practically with one very large bed in the middle, two chests, and a small table and two chairs arranged in front of the large hearth.

"Why is your laird such an unhappy man, Moyra?" Rather than turn around, she continued her perusal of the room, staring at the assortment of swords and dirks on the wall. She couldn't decide what exactly gave her the feeling, but something seemed terribly wrong here. It was as if thoughts and memories weighed down everyone in the clan. It was different than the mood in the Merrill keep. There, the servants moved in fear of their laird; here, the people seemed to revere the MacGregor laird. And yet there was an underlying sadness to that respect, something she couldn't quite comprehend. She'd never experienced the like in her sire's keep or her husband's.

"My laird was a good lad. He and his brothers have had a difficult life."

"How long have ye been here?"

"I have always been with the MacGregors. I was here with Lady MacGregor when each of the lads was born." Moyra bustled around the chamber as they spoke, arranging linen strips and basins, towels for Catherine's bath. They stopped their conversation when three lads brought in several buckets of steaming water and dumped them into the tub.

"How many brothers are there?"

Moyra closed the door after the lads left and motioned

for Catherine to join her by the tub. Together, they removed Catherine's dirty trews. Moyra clucked when she saw the damage to her legs and her knees, then untied the strip of plaid from her foot and examined it from side to side. Her gaze traveled back to Catherine's knees again, and she let out a deep sigh as if she suspected what had caused those bruises. "These are a bit older, but no matter. I'll clean everything a bit so the water won't be so red from the blood. Then you may bathe and I'll apply a poultice and wrap your wounds afterward."

Catherine noticed Moyra hadn't answered her last question, so she tried a different tactic. "I've heard the laird is cold-hearted. Is he?"

"My laird? Nay, he is tender-hearted, he just hides it behind his anger."

"His anger?" Catherine had to probe further. She wished to find out what drove the man. What had happened here?

"Aye. Are ye not from this part of the Highlands? Everyone knows of the attack on the MacGregors seven years ago."

"I have always lived in the Highlands, but I do not hear much news from outside my keep. Please tell me. What happened?"

"We were attacked by someone we thought to be an ally," Moyra said as she tended to Catherine's hurts. "They came in the middle of the night, killed our laird, our mistress, and their eldest lad." The older woman's eyes misted as she told the story, and she squeezed them tightly shut at the end as if she could banish the memories from her mind. Catherine was shocked to hear of such a travesty. All she'd ever heard from the Merrills was that the MacGregors were daft and cruel.

It dawned on her that Moyra spoke of Graeme's family.

"He lost his parents and his brother all in the same day?" How awful for the man, a tragedy that one could never get past if she were to guess.

"Aye." Having finished her ministrations, Moyra helped Catherine into the tub and then took a seat in a nearby chair. "Aye, 'twas the worst day of my life. I was hiding a short distance away with two of the lads, but Graeme and Boyd were close at hand. Still, I was peeking through the door to the courtyard when it happened, and I saw what those poor boys saw. They watched their mother die, then their brother, and finally their sire. The memory is burned into all of our minds. I cannae imagine how it felt for those poor lads. Graeme lives his life for the sole purpose of revenge, and who could blame him?"

"How many brothers does he have?"

"Four survived—Graeme, Conn, Boyd, and Rory. Alpin was killed. Boyd never recovered from what he saw that day." Her hands fell into her lap. "I pray every day for some happiness to come into our laird's life, but the Lord has not deemed it time yet."

Catherine felt guilty asking the old woman to relive such painful memories, but she could not help herself. Something told her this was important. She used the cloth to wash her face, then turned to stare at Moyra. "Who? Who committed such an atrocity?"

Moyra lifted her gaze to Catherine's and whispered. "Henry Merrill. Surely you've heard of the cruel bastard." She stopped to cross herself and then lowered her head in prayer.

Catherine dropped the soap she held into the water, grateful that Moyra had turned away and could not see the expression of shock on her face. Her own husband was the guilty party.

Catherine gulped and picked up the soap again, blindly

washing her arms. "Henry Merrill? It was him? Are you sure it was not his men instead?" She did her best to hide the trembling of her hands, shoving them under the water.

Moyra's face swiveled toward her. "I saw it with my own eyes. I hid the lads behind me, but I watched him take his sword and slice across my lady's sweet neck." She burst into tears. "I could not watch anymore. 'Twas too painful. But Graeme? He watched it all. Why the devil spared him, no one knows. But Graeme lives for revenge against the Merrill."

Catherine could not believe her ears. Henry was a murderer. He'd murdered a woman and a child in cold blood. Her mind launched in ten different directions at this revelation. If her husband was such a cruel, violent man, what would prevent him from killing her? Killing Issy? She had to get her daughter and escape from him for good.

A loud knock echoed through the chamber. Moyra answered it and stepped outside to speak to whomever was outside the door.

It was just as well because Catherine's thoughts had spiraled out of control. The healing of her child was no longer her primary concern. She needed to get Issy safe. Where could they go? She hated her sire, Clyde Beaton. She'd never return to him. He was the one who'd given her to the Merrill, and he'd likely as not send her back.

Why hadn't the king punished Henry for his crimes? She had to find out. Something was wrong, very wrong. She stepped out of the tub and covered herself with the linen towel Moyra had set out, drying her skin and checking her wounds at the same time. She had one ragged tear on her right thigh, probably from the boar's teeth when he'd jumped at her, and there were several smaller wounds on her left foot, though none as deep as the one on her thigh. The leather boot had protected her for sure. Her knees had improved.

The only problem was that her left foot, while not badly mangled, was quite swollen from being twisted. Her ankle pained her terribly when she walked on it. As much as she wished to run out of this keep and do what she could to save Issy, as fearful as she was about what Henry would do when he discovered she was gone, she had to stay—for two reasons. She needed to heal her ankle, and she needed to find out the full story about the attack.

"Come sit down," Moyra said with a kindly smile. "I'll apply the poultice and wrap your wounds."

Catherine sat in the chair and extended her leg. "May I ask ye a question about healing?"

"Aye. I'm not too skilled, but I know more than many."

"Have you heard of an illness that makes a child sickly? One that makes her tire too much when she's up and about? One that makes her so fatigued as to not leave her bed?" Unsure of how else to describe Issy's symptoms, she stumbled for more words, but came up with nothing sensible.

Moyra asked, "Does she carry the fever? Have a wound?"

Catherine thought for a moment. Had her daughter ever had a fever? "Nay, not that I recall, and no wound."

Moyra paused, clearly deep in thought, but then shook her head. "Nay, I cannae say I've seen such. 'Tis so rare for a wee one not to be full of energy. The lads were all so hard to control until tragedy struck. Graeme's sire took them outside all the time because they were too busy for my lady. But he loved his lads so. It saddened me that she never had a daughter, but now I understand why the Lord did not gift her with a daughter. What would have happened to a sweet lass in the hands of Henry Merrill?"

Catherine's thoughts became more jumbled. *What, indeed?* All these revelations had caused her head to pound miserably. "Moyra, I'd like to lie down for a wee bit if you dinnae mind." She'd rest a bit, then decide what to do next. Should she go for the healer or go back? She trusted Dolag and Margaret to protect and care for Issy, but did they know of Henry's tendencies?

"Nay. Go ahead and rest. You must be exhausted after such an attack." Moyra helped her settle on the bed and covered her with a pile of furs.

She sank into the soft mattress and huddled under the covers. Never had Catherine slept in such a comfortable bed as the laird's. Unfortunately, her mind continued to race with thoughts about her husband and fear for her daughter.

One thing continued to echo in her mind. What was the truth? Perhaps there was something she needed to do before she left. She had to trust that Margaret, Benneit, and her maid would watch over her daughter a bit longer. She had to stay to find out the truth about her husband.

Graeme couldn't get the flame-haired siren out of his mind. Never had he been so entranced with a woman before. *A married woman*, he reminded himself yet again. He'd ridden hard after leaving the keep, hoping to catch up with his men. Though he didn't care to admit it, part of his haste was his need to get away from the beauty in trews. She affected his thinking, and he needed to regain his focus.

The Merrill was his priority. His original plan had been to move to his land and kill everyone inside his curtain wall—man, woman, or child.

But Boyd's words had resonated with him because he'd been having the same thoughts. If he could only talk to his sire, gain his guidance, but it wasn't to be.

He had to be objective and take his emotion out of this. Henry Merrill had killed his mother, his father, and his brother in front of him. It was only fitting that he do the same for him. Did his parents live with him? According to what they'd learned on their scouting missions, the man did not live with his parents, but he did have a wife and child, and a sister. It seemed appropriate that he should kill the Merrill's wife and child in front of him, then kill the Merrill. He was uncertain about the sister.

Since it would be an attack, there would be casualties. Merrill's warriors would die, just as many MacGregor warriors had lost their lives in the long-ago attack. This also was fitting.

He had to agree with Boyd. He would not kill everyone.

His warriors would be forced to accept his decision. He, as laird, had the right to change his orders—to choose to be a more humane leader than Henry Merrill. Boyd wanted it, Conn wanted it, and it would set a good example for Rory. He would have to inform his men that his instructions had changed.

He hadn't traveled far when he came upon Conn and Rory. "How did ye fare? Did ye uncover the information we sought?" His jaw clenched tight as he awaited their response.

Conn spoke first. "We uncovered more than expected, but I'd prefer to discuss it at our keep."

Graeme nodded to his brother. "We'll meet in my solar as soon as we return." He turned his horse around and headed back toward his castle, leading his men.

Rory shouted to him. "How does the lady fare?"

If Graeme answered truly, he'd tell him the lady fared beautifully, but he did not care to let on that he had any feelings for her. "The woman, or lady, is with Moyra at present, getting her wounds tended. They were worse than I had realized. The boar would have killed her. I came upon her just in time."

"But she'll live?" Rory asked.

Graeme glanced over his shoulder at Rory. He had a soft spot for the lad because he reminded him of their father. Rory's hair was both brown and red—brown like their father's and red like their mother's—depending on where he stood. He did not know where his own dark locks came from. All his brothers had brown hair except for Rory, whose locks were redder. "She will live."

"Do ye know where she was traveling?"

"Nay, but I'll find out before she leaves," Graeme replied as a small smile crept across his face. He would enjoy cajoling the information from her, even if, or *especially* if, she spouted fire at him.

"You'll not hurt her, will ye, Graeme?"

Rory was young enough to still have a soft heart. Perhaps Graeme found him so endearing because he was so different from the rest of them. He had no memory of their parents' death, while Conn and Boyd were both haunted by the past.

As was he.

"Nay, Rory. I do not hurt innocent women."

Conn asked, "What if she isnae innocent?"

Graeme jerked his head around to look his brother in the eye. "Say what ye mean. What have ye learned of the lass?"

"It may be nothing," Conn replied, holding out his hand palm up. "I know not who the tale is about."

"What tale?" Now Conn had piqued his curiosity.

"I'll inform ye in your solar." Conn had the most serious expression on his face. His brother's insistence that they wait to have the conversation in private was curious, but he nodded in agreement. They had plenty of time to discuss the implications of all they had learned on their small scouting venture.

Once inside the solar, Graeme sat behind his desk while Tomag, Conn, and Rory grabbed chairs to sit down. As soon as they were settled, he asked, "How many men?"

"Everything we've seen on this visit supports our previous assessment," Conn replied. "I would say he has around one hundred warriors and another hundred men who work the land and do not fight with his warriors except when Henry is desperate. They could always be trained and added to Merrill's numbers, but they've little experience in the lists."

"And the other information you wished to tell me?" His brother fell silent. Conn glanced at Rory, then at Tomag, who finally spoke.

"My guess is this would not be the best time to plan an attack."

Graeme set his elbows on his desk, leaning toward his second in command. "Why no'?"

Conn took over for Tomag. "Because his men arenae all there, and I worry that he could leave at any time, something he rarely does. Ye dinnae wish to attack if he's no' there. Cowardly man that he is, he'd take the chance to run off. Word has it that several search parties have been sent off his land."

"Why?" Graeme pressed, anxious for them to continue.

Tomag nodded at Conn, who cleared his throat and whispered, "Because someone is missing."

"Who?" Graeme asked.

"His wife. She went missing about ten hours ago."

Graeme's eyes widened. "They're searching the area for Merrill's wife?"

Tomag added, "Aye. Merrill's wife has disappeared."

CHAPTER FIVE

G RAEME'S HEAD NEARLY EXPLODED. THIS was no coincidence. Catherine had to be the Merrill's wife. Once he got over the shock, his brain jumped in a hundred directions. Oh, he could use this to his benefit, but he'd have to give it careful thought.

He stood from his desk.

"Graeme, do ye think she's Merrill's wife?" Rory whispered.

"I dinnae know for sure, but I'll find out. Tomag, ask Moyra to bring Catherine to me."

Rory asked again, "You'll nae hurt her, will you?"

"As I've told ye before, I dinnae hurt innocent women or bairns."

"*Is* she innocent?" Conn asked, crossing his arms in front of him. So, *this* was what he'd implied when they were on the road earlier. "Who knows what she's done?"

"For one, she's in league with the devil. How could she be married to such a cruel bastard?" Graeme hadn't realized he'd spoken the words aloud.

"Mayhap she was forced," Rory replied. "Mayhap she was running away from him because he's so cruel. Ye need to find out the truth, Graeme."

Graeme's mind was whirling. Was Catherine truly Henry Merrill's wife? If so, was she aware of the brutal massacre her husband had committed on MacGregor land? Was she one of the ones who had convinced the king that the attack had been mounted by one of Merrill's men—and not Merrill himself?

They'd gone to the king after hearing rumors of the Merrill's lies. The king had substantiated the story: Henry Merrill claimed that one of his best warriors had gone daft, recruited a few of Merrill's men, and then mounted the attack on the MacGregors. Merrill vowed he'd had no knowledge of the traitor. His only reason for venturing onto MacGregor land, according to him, was because someone had been stealing his cattle, and he'd hoped to find the guilty party. Instead, he'd discovered what his warriors had done—and had them killed.

The king had believed his lies.

Graeme had vowed not to let the fear of retaliation stop him. This was justice, and he had witnesses to attest to what the Merrill had done. He could not allow the possibility of the king's anger to stop him. Conn and Rory had tried to talk him into approaching the king for his blessing, but he and Tomag had agreed it was too dangerous. The Merrill might learn of their plans, and he would not risk it.

He'd deal with the king *after* he served justice with his own sword.

The door opened and Tomag stepped aside to allow Catherine to enter. Graeme stood, and his breath caught when he realized she was dressed in one of his mother's gowns—a dark red garment that matched her hair perfectly. Brocade decorated the top of the bodice that clung to her curves.

No one spoke for a few moments until Catherine

cleared her throat and stared at her feet, her hands clasped in front of her.

Graeme, unable to tear his gaze from the vision in front of him, said to the others, "Leave us."

Conn, Rory, and Tomag turned to leave, though Rory cast one last glance over his shoulder before he left.

"Please be seated, Catherine." Graeme pointed to a chair and she sat, settling her skirts carefully around her.

"Catherine Merrill, is it not?"

She closed her eyes and let out a deep breath, nodding her head almost imperceptibly. "Aye. How did ye find out?"

"We were headed to Merrill land when I found you. I sent the men ahead." His head was spinning. It horrified him to think she was married to his enemy, but it also meant she was an unbelievable asset. She knew the Merrill's castle, the keep, probably even the tunnels underneath.

How aware was she of her husband's activities? Of his warriors? Of his plans?

Graeme could imprison her and force the laird to come to his land, then kill him and his warriors as soon as they arrived.

The possibilities were endless. He needed to tread carefully and plan accordingly.

He pulled a dirk from the wall behind him and started to flip it in his hand. "Your husband has many search parties out for you. Ye did not inform him ye were leaving?"

She lifted her chin and stared at the wall, refusing to look at him. "Nay. I snuck out when he was gone."

"Why?"

"I dinnae think 'tis your concern."

"I think it *is* my concern."

When she turned her gaze back to him, the fire he'd

seen there earlier was back. Damn, but she was breath-taking. He adjusted himself behind the desk because his cock had sprung to life again, much as he hated to admit it. Knowing who she was should have changed all his feel-ings, transformed his curiosity to hatred. What control did this woman have over him? He shoved his chair back and stood, spinning around to hide his erection. He ran his hand across his face to wipe the sweat that had exploded on his forehead. Getting himself under control was para-mount. No woman had ever affected him this way.

"Because ye think he killed your family? I have never heard of such a thing. I cannae believe 'tis true."

Her voice brought him back to the conversation at hand, and he was finally able to turn around without embarrass-ing himself. Her green gaze caught his immediately.

"How did ye learn of my family?" he asked. "Were ye married to him then?" Certainly it was possible, but she appeared too young to have been married for seven years or more. He returned to his chair and twirled the dirk in his hand, hoping she'd say nay, hoping she'd had nothing to do with Henry Merrill then. Why? Why did he wish for her innocence?

"Moyra informed me. I married the Merrill six years ago. Though I heard about a tragedy involving your clan before I wed him, I've never heard it mentioned at our castle. I cannae believe he would commit such a horren-dous act. I do not *want* to believe it."

"Do ye love your husband?"

She snorted, and he couldn't stop a smile from creeping across his face. "Nay. There is no love between us."

"Do ye trust your husband?"

"Nay." She stared at her lap, fiddling with her fingers. "Nay. I hate my husband."

The relief that radiated through him was surprising.

He wanted her innocence, which required that she be unhappy with her marriage. "Is that why ye left?"

"In part." Her gaze shifted to the side wall, staring at the weapons there.

He could see she fought tears. "And the other reason ye left?"

She shook her head as a tear escaped and slid down her cheek. She reached up to swipe it away. "Ye dinnae need to know."

He sighed and leaned forward on his desk. "Nay. I may not. But I am not the monster your husband is. Mayhap I can help you."

She shook her head, the tears now flowing freely.

"Catherine, I would guess he is a cruel man in all his dealings. If he has abused ye in any way, I will protect you. Has he beaten you?"

Catherine couldn't stop her tears. Graeme wished to *help* her. This man in front of her was so unlike the other men in her life. Her sire, her husband, both had always barked at her, ordered her about, told her everything they found unsuitable. She was not allowed to talk to any of the men in the castle other than Benneit. Indeed, her husband forbade her to talk with *anyone* other than his sister and the servants assigned to her. Even if she had been allowed to speak freely, she never would have had the courage to speak to a man the way she spoke to Graeme MacGregor. She spoke her mind to him without fear of retaliation. Why? He was such a contradiction to everything she'd learned in her life…

Suddenly, she felt as though she should tell him all—the beatings, the ridicule, even about her daughter.

She brought her gaze up to his, doing her best to stop

her sniffling. His blue eyes warmed her insides. She needed to trust someone, and some instinct told her she could trust this man.

"Aye, I have suffered beatings at his hand." She blushed, embarrassed to openly admit it. "I have not given him the sons he wants, so he punishes me. I believe he delights in coming up with new punishments." She stood up and lifted her skirts, being beyond modesty at this point.

He quirked his brow at her, but then he noticed the wounds on her knees, which were *not* from the boar's attack. She knew the exact moment he saw them because his eyes lit with fury. Somehow, she knew it was not directed at her. She dropped her skirts and sat down. "Those came from a punishment because I had my courses again—and because he has been unable to perform. He claims this is entirely my fault. I know little about such things, but even I know if he cannot perform, I willnae be carrying, yet he blames it all on me."

"And this is why you left…to find help?"

She stared at her hands in her lap. Such a thought had never occurred to her. She'd always thought it to be the way of the world. Her sire had hit her mother many times. He'd beat the help, too. She hadn't thought she'd ever be treated any differently.

"Nay. I left because we have a daughter of four sum-mers, and she has been ill for almost a year. She weakens more and more every day." She paused to wipe fresh tears again. "I fear I shall lose her, and Isbeil is the reason I wish to live. She is the love of my life, yet he will do nothing to help her. He has no reputable healer."

"Most sires would send for every healer in the land to tend their child. He does not care about her well-being?"

"Nay. He never visits her, but I don't complain about it. He has not seen her in so long, I know not if she would recognize him, and I'd prefer for her to never know her sire. He is too cruel, and I fear when she is older, he'll start punishing her for the slightest transgressions. I do my best not to mention him to her. Only his mother reminds Isbeil of her sire."

"So ye wish to help your ill daughter. Where were you headed? Home?"

"Nay. My sire is no better than Henry Merrill. A healer on the outskirts of our land was known to be talented. I thought if I could reach her, she could tell me what to do, tell me something that would help her. I cannot stand by and watch my daughter die."

He took a deep breath and let it out slowly. "You've put me in a difficult situation." He turned his chair and stared at the weapons on the wall, drilling his fingers on the desk.

"I do not understand how that could be. I will be on my way soon."

"You've been honest with me, so I will do the same. My goal in life has been to seek revenge on your husband. Whether ye choose to believe it or not, I watched him kill three of my family members. He will pay. Now that I hear how he treats you, do ye doubt that he could commit such a heinous crime? I hear nothing good about the man."

She dropped her gaze to her hands in her lap, embarrassed to be married to such a cruel man. "Nay, while at first I was caught by surprise, I cannae deny he is capable of such an atrocity if he feels he has justification, whatever that may be in his mind. How have I put you in a difficult situation?"

"Because I will repay the man by taking his life. I also planned to take the lives of all of his family, including his wife and any children he has sired."

She gasped and stared at him wide-eyed.

"I see you have discovered my meaning. You have given me the perfect solution. I could kill you and take your body to him to start the war."

"Please, nay! Isbeil needs me."

"I could kill her, too." He never flinched when he spoke of killing.

Could Moyra have been so wrong about him? Could he be as cold-hearted as she'd heard? How could a man capable of gentleness, as she knew him to be, commit such terrible sins?

She shook her head, unable to speak any words but one. "*Please.*"

He stood and moved to sit on the front of his desk, tugging her out of her chair to stand in front of him. When they were eye-to-eye, he took hold of her hands. "For some reason, ye have captured my interest." He brushed the back of his hand across her cheek. "Ye have suffered at his hands just as my people have. So I promise ye that I will not take your life or your daughter's. I will make no such promise about your husband. He will die at my hand."

He stared into her eyes and her belly fluttered, heat shooting from the skin he touched straight to her core. She did not understand it, but she liked it.

He stared at her cheek, bringing his hand up to a sore spot where the skin was broken, rubbing his thumb across it. "Did your husband do this to ye?"

"Aye, he slapped me, and he wears a heavy ring. He has done so many times." She blushed. Her husband had always blamed her for his ill treatment, and while she had never quite believed it, the words had sunk in deep.

Graeme MacGregor made her question everything.

Despite herself, she wished for more from this man—

more touches, more tenderness. The warmth in his eyes, which had been so cold moments ago, mesmerized her.

He took her by complete surprise as his lips descended on hers. She froze, his lips warm, soft, and enticing.

He pulled back and whispered, "Ye do not like to be kissed? I care not that ye are married. I want you."

"I've never been kissed like that. My husband doesnae kiss me."

He smiled and cupped her cheeks. "Allow me to teach you." He kissed her again, showing a tenderness that confused her.

She leaned into him, enjoying the new sensations coursing through her body at his taste and his touch. She'd never enjoyed any physical contact with her husband, but kissing Graeme was wondrous. He teased her lips with his tongue and she parted them, allowing him inside, giving him permission to taste her as she did him.

A small moan crept from the back of Catherine's throat, surprising her, but it was her natural response to the heat that traveled through her, making her feel more alive than ever. One moment she shivered and the next she melted against him. His mouth angled over hers as he deepened the kiss, ravaging her mouth in a way that spread new sensations through her, and her knees buckled in response to his sweet assault.

He ended the kiss and the corners of his mouth curled up into a sweet smile. "Ye are a fine student, a quick learner." He kissed her quickly and then stood up from the desk. "Ye have given me much to think about, lass, but I will keep my word."

"What will ye do with me?"

"I have not decided yet, but know this. Ye are mine to protect. I will protect ye and your daughter, when I find her, with my life."

"Ye will go after her? For me?" She was stunned by this declaration. Hope blossomed in her heart. She had spent the last hours worried about her daughter's safety in the Merrill keep—had she found a solution so easily?

"Not yet. I must have a plan. But know this—your husband will die at the end of my sword. If this upsets you, so be it, I will not apologize. He will reap what he sowed. When we attack his castle, I will do my best to bring your daughter back to you."

"But I must return to her. When will ye attack? I cannae be away from her for more than a few days. I must go to the healer first, and then return to her."

"Our plan is to attack within a fortnight. I cannae allow ye to return and tell him our plans. Lass, I'm sorry. When we attack, I will search out your daughter and return her to you."

"A fortnight?" The thought of leaving Issy alone for so long, cared for only by Rodina, made her weak and dizzy. "'Tis too long…I cannae leave her…" True, Margaret and Dolag would watch over her, but she'd never been away from her daughter before.

"Ye have no choice. I will lock ye here if I must. I willnae risk jeopardizing what we have planned for years."

She grasped his hand, clutching it to her chest. She had to make him understand about Issy. Something… anything… "Take me with ye. I can help ye. There must be some way I can be of assistance. You'll not know where Issy is kept. I must show you."

He loosened her grip on his hand and cocooned it inside his own. "Mayhap ye can help me. Could ye draw a map of the castle? Can ye tell me about the outbuildings in your bailey? Do ye know where the tunnel is beneath your castle?"

Her face fell. Her husband kept many details from her.

Panic settled over her as the reality of her predicament settled on her. "I know little. I can show ye some of the castle, but not all. The same with the outbuildings." Tears blurred her vision. "I know nothing of any tunnel." She could feel her heartbeat speed up at the hopelessness of her situation.

"You mentioned his mother. How many of his family live with him? Does his sire still live?"

"Nay, his mother lives and a sister. His mother is much like him, but his sister is as sweet as can be."

"Any other bairns?"

"He has a nephew. Margaret has a son named Wesley." She bit her lip, wondering if she would regret giving him this information. "He is only six summers, and he is not at all like my husband."

"What about the lad's sire? Does he live?" His narrowed gaze told her how much calculating and planning was going on behind his eyes.

"Nay, he is dead. That is all he has besides Issy and me. Please, you must spare Margaret and Wesley. He is a sweet lad, and she has helped me many times, defending me to her brother."

She caught the slight curve in his mouth. "You do not defend his mother, I notice."

Staring at her hands again, she did not know how to answer him. She had no feelings for Rodina.

"Your silence speaks volumes."

A deafening silence sat between them as Graeme took in all this information, the only sound she heard was from the small dagger still flipping in his hand.

"Do ye know how many men he has prepared to do battle? Do ye know of any weak points in his curtain wall?"

She shook her head. "Not for certes. Mayhap one hundred? Six score?" Her breath hitched. She had to get back to Issy, she just had to. Another thought occurred to her. "You'll not kill the others? My maid? My manservant? My husband's dear sister is not at all like him. You'll spare her and her son?"

"I cannae promise about your husband's sister or the manservant. That I'll not know until we arrive. Most of the men will likely die. I will save you, but my warriors and my people need to feel justice has been served. His family for mine." His voice softened as his gaze caught hers. "Your husband's nephew could be considered a fair exchange for my brother."

She stared at him, tears cresting over her lids at the implications of all he'd said. Had she not left, he could have been planning to kill all of them, including sweet Issy. Is that why she'd been so compelled to leave at the time she did? Had fate sent her into the path of Graeme MacGregor for a reason?

"Please think on all I've asked. I'll find ye materials to sketch a map for us."

Her mind worked feverishly, trying to think of anything she knew that could help him. She was worried for Margaret, for little Wes, and for the men who worked around the castle. Some of them, she knew, were good. Yet there was no denying the hope that surged in her heart. Henry would finally be stopped. "I know…I know the back entrance to the curtain wall. Take me along and I'll lead ye there. Please?"

A knock sounded at the door, and he stepped out to answer it. She tried to listen but could not understand their conversation. The sound was too muted by the door, but Graeme finally opened it, and she heard his last words.

"Rory, wait here and I'll send her with you."

When he stepped back inside the door, the coldness had

returned to his eyes.

"Your husband's men are searching for you. I expect they may come to my land soon. You must stay inside my chamber while I speak with my brother and my second to determine our next steps. I warn ye not to come out for any reason. If we're not careful, ye may bring a clan war down on us without any way to protect your daughter."

"Aye."

He took two steps closer. "Will ye do that for me? Promise to stay hidden no matter what ye hear? I'll give ye the tools ye need to draw the map. Write down all ye can remember."

When he stood so close, the heat of his body warmed her, a luxury she'd not had often. "Aye, I will hide as long as you promise me that you will save my daughter." She lifted her gaze to his. She had to get his promise, or she would not draw the map.

"You have my word, but only when the timing is right. We will not go onto Merrill's land blind. Help us learn as much as we can." He kissed her forehead and whispered, "Go now."

Rory knocked and opened the door. "My lady, I shall take you to my laird's chamber. 'Tis the safest of all."

She followed Rory to Graeme's chamber. Before he left her there, the lad said, "My lady, promise me you will not tell my laird, but if we are attacked, I fear for your life." His voice dropped to a whisper. "If ye believe we are being attacked, there is a door under the rug in the corner. 'Twill take you through a tunnel and into the middle of the forest. No one will be there. I will come for you."

Fear cut Catherine to the core. Had it really come to this? What would happen to her and her daughter?

CHAPTER SIX

L ATER THAT EVENING, CATHERINE SNUCK out of Graeme's chamber, hoping to explore a bit. The door to the chamber opposite her was ajar, so she crept over to peek inside. A young lad sat at a table, staring at something in front of him. Hadn't Moyra mentioned a brother who had never recovered from the tragedy?

Something compelled her to knock on the door. The lad popped out of his chair, wide-eyed, but said nothing.

"Greetings. My name is Catherine. Who are you?"

After a long pause, he motioned her inside the chamber and pointed to the chair across from him at the table, so she sat down and folded her hands in her lap.

"What's your name?" she asked.

His eyes never left hers, but he did not answer.

"Are ye Graeme's brother?"

After a short pause, he nodded, giving her a small smile.

He was a handsome boy with brown hair and blue eyes like his brother, but his eyes were different—haunted in a way that saddened her.

She stared at her hands for a moment, but then whispered, "My apologies for what my husband did to your clan."

The boy stood up so fast, he knocked the chair over. Fear and hatred filled his gaze in an instant.

She stood and followed him, reaching for his arm. "Nay, I'll not hurt you. I promise." She noticed how his hand shook as soon as she touched his wrist, but he did not pull away. Seven years ago, this boy would have been a wee lad—much too young to watch his parents die in front of him. How agonizing that day must have been for him. All these years later, he was still suffering. Tears brimmed in her eyes. "My husband is a beast. I was not married to him at the time, and I knew nothing of this tragedy until I came here. Your brother…"

He leaned toward her.

"Graeme saved me from a boar's attack. I was…well, 'tis not important why I was there, but your brother rescued me just as the boar was about to take a large bite out of my leg."

He laughed and whispered, "Boyd."

"Boyd? 'Tis you? 'Tis a pleasure to know ye, lad."

He pointed to her leg.

"Aye, I am still limping from the injury in the forest. It would have been much worse if Graeme had not come along."

Boyd whispered, "Graeme is good. Takes care of us." He pointed to the door.

She spun around to see Graeme leaning against the side of the door, his arms crossed in front of him. He did not look happy.

Graeme couldn't believe what he was hearing. His brothers had tried for years to talk to Boyd, but Catherine had strolled into his chamber—uninvited—and gained his trust in a matter of moments. The lass had bewitched

Boyd as fast as she had him.

As soon as Catherine noticed him, he pushed away from the door and closed it behind him. He did not want it known that Boyd had paid Catherine a courtesy he had not yet extended to their brothers. "Boyd, you've met my new friend, Catherine."

Boyd smiled at Catherine, but then his expression turned serious. "Catherine Merrill."

Graeme clasped his shoulder and said, "Aye, Catherine Merrill."

"You saved her, Graeme."

"I guess I did. Are ye angry with me because she's the Merrill's wife?"

Boyd shook his head. "Was not her fault."

Graeme glanced at Catherine, presently wringing her hands in front of her. "Nay, 'twas not her fault."

"Henry Merrill's fault."

"Aye," Graeme whispered.

Boyd turned to Catherine and whispered, "I saw him kill my mother. I closed my eyes for the rest. Graeme helped me."

Catherine stammered, but much to her credit, she did not shy away from Boyd. "No lad should have to see such a thing. I am sorry that ye and your brothers had to watch and that ye suffered such a loss."

Boyd turned to Graeme. "I'm tired now."

Catherine started. "Would ye like help getting into bed? I'll help ye with the covers."

Boyd nodded.

Graeme watched as Catherine helped Boyd into bed, admiring her gentleness. She surprised him again when she bent to kiss the lad's forehead before she left.

Graeme snuffed the candles and followed her out of the chamber. "I'll be here to visit on the morrow, Boyd," he said before closing the door.

But Boyd had already fallen asleep. He looked almost… content.

Once they were alone in the hall, Catherine turned to him. "I did not mean to pry. I knocked and he invited me in."

"Catherine, ye are only the second person he has spoken with in seven years. I dinnae fault ye, I thank ye."

She looked taken aback, and for a moment she didn't say anything at all. Finally, she broke the silence. "You've all had such terrible tragedy in your lives, and 'tis all my husband's fault. I know not what to say."

"Just say you'll help us. Ye know things we do not." He cupped her cheek and brushed his thumb across her soft skin. This woman was unlike any he'd ever met.

"I'll help however I can. I promise."

Graeme spent the night on the floor in the great hall, giving Catherine his bed. He did not disturb her, though he wanted nothing more than to climb into his bed and enjoy her until she screamed his name in passion. But he needed some distance to think, to ensure he had considered every possible scenario now that he had Merrill's wife in his castle. After a few early hours of practice in the lists, he headed to the tower and rushed up the staircase, Conn following.

"What are ye doin'?" Conn yelled up to him.

"I'm going to the ramparts. I think the best when I'm standing in front of the parapets."

Moments later, they were standing side by side on the cold stone curtain wall. Graeme leaned against the parapets and studied his land.

"What are ye lookin' for?" Conn asked.

"The Merrills. Tomag said they are searching everywhere for her."

"Do ye think the Merrill has the bollocks to show up here?"

"Nay, *he* will not, but he will send his men. I see no one yet." He crossed his arms and leaned back against the stone wall of the tower. "I have a decision to make."

"What decision?"

Graeme stared at him. "Ye cannae guess?"

His brother chewed on his thumbnail, something he'd done since he was a wee lad. "Aye. Ye need to decide what to do with Catherine. What ideas have ye considered? I'd like to hear them, mayhap share some ideas of my own."

What would he do without Conn by his side? He tried not to think on it much. His brother kept him focused, level-headed. "I've had several," he answered. "The obvious is to take her to the Merrill and kill her in cold blood as he did our mother, but I cannae do it." It would be an eye-for-an-eye, but he could not bear to do it. Conn would agree with this choice. He'd tried many times to convince him to spare the women and children.

"I'm pleased to hear ye finally admit that." His brother tipped his chin up, as if daring Graeme to disagree with him.

Graeme turned his head to stare out over his land again, knowing his brother was right. Now that he knew her, had tasted her, he would not be able to take her life. "Nay, I cannae take an innocent woman's life."

"Ye believe she had no knowledge of what happened here?"

"Aye, she is innocent."

"And that is your head talking and not your cock?"

Graeme swung his head back to stare at his brother, surprised at his boldness. He grinned and said, "Aye, 'tis my head speaking. Catherine is a beautiful woman, but that does nae change my goal. I will kill her husband and his warriors. She has convinced me to spare the children. She has a daughter who is everything to her. The lady bears only hatred for her husband, but 'tis not why she was running. Her daughter is sickly and the villain refuses to do anything to help her."

"How old is the daughter?"

"Four summers. I believe her. She has a fiery nature when she speaks of her daughter. And why else would a woman venture alone across the Highlands?"

"Your other thoughts?" Conn's hands went to his hips, waiting to hear his other thoughts on the matter.

"I'll not kill the women either. The clan doesn't know yet."

"That pleases me, also. Your men will do as ye instruct when the time is nigh."

Graeme mulled over whether or not to share everything with Conn, but then decided to be completely honest with him. "His mother lives with him. He also has a sister and her son."

Conn's face registered exactly what he had hoped. He waited for him to process what he'd said.

"The son would be heir since Catherine only has a daughter…" Conn rubbed his face, then stared at Graeme.

"Aye. You've come upon the dilemma."

"For this attack to be just, the clan will expect ye to take the lives of the Merrill, his wife, and his first heir."

"Aye, but his first heir is six summers old. I dinnae think I'm capable of taking the life of one so young, but I must."

Conn meant more to Graeme than anyone, but while he trusted his brother's good judgment, he was not certain Conn understood his drive. Only he and Boyd had seen the Merrill kill their parents and eldest brother. Still, he needed Conn to support his plan. True, as laird he could command all of his brothers and clanspeople to follow his instructions, but he wanted his brother's approval.

He decided it was best to tell him everything that had crossed his mind. "I've had several thoughts about what we should do with Catherine, but I've already dismissed many. Would ye like to hear them all?"

"Aye, I would. Go ahead."

"When the Merrill's men come, we can advise them we hold Catherine for ransom. Our price is for Henry Merrill to come to us unarmed. 'Twould give me great pleasure to spill his blood on MacGregor land."

"A possibility that could bring harm to Catherine."

"Aye, which is why 'tis no' my first choice." Graeme paced the parapets. "Another possibility is simply to release her and continue on with our original plan."

"Are ye sure she willnae go back and tell her husband of our plan?"

"Nay, not willingly. He beats her, though, so he could beat it out of her. 'Tis not my first choice either. I cannae knowingly send her to such a fate."

He paused, a plethora of ideas bouncing in and out of his mind.

"A slight twist on that plan would be to return her and ask her to get information for us. Then I will return to the Merrill's keep alone to meet with her."

"Can she no' give ye this information now?"

"Nay, she says not. She says she doesnae know the entire structure of the keep, or the number of warriors he commands, but she is drawing a map for me. She knows where the back entrance to the curtain wall sits. I am not surprised the Merrill kept much from her. However, she could attempt to retrieve more information for us if we send her back. I believe she would." He rubbed his hand across the back of his neck, hating that he had such an important decision to make—and that he no longer felt like he could make his choice without considering Catherine's well-being.

"Would you take her back yourself? What reason would you give the Merrill? He willnae believe you have good intentions."

"I agree. I would tell him that we ask for peace and no further troubles from the Merrill clan."

Conn shook his head. "He'll not agree to that, nor believe it."

"I cannae say ye are wrong. Remember that I am giving ye all the possibilities that have crossed my mind." He paced and turned again. "I've considered taking her with us on the attack so we can save her daughter."

"Ye dinnae like that choice?"

"Nay. I dinnae wish to risk her life. One arrow from the curtain wall would kill her." He ran his hand through his hair and chewed on his lip. There was only one choice left to him, but he doubted Conn would agree with it. Nonetheless, it was the choice he leaned toward. He thought it his best chance for a complete revenge.

Conn asked, "What is it? Ye have another idea?"

"Aye. Ye willnae like it, but 'tis my preference."

"Go ahead." He crossed his arms and pursed his lips, waiting for him to speak.

Graeme paused in his pacing and then stopped directly in front of his brother. "I think we should continue on as planned. I'll take what information she can offer, use it, but I'll leave her behind."

"Why?"

"She doesnae wish to stay there. She hates her husband, and my plan is to end his life, so why should she return?"

"Ye just told me she has a daughter."

"Aye, and I plan to bring her daughter to her. I promised Catherine as much. 'Twas the only way I could get her to reveal what she knows."

"She may have others she wishes to protect."

"She does. Merrill's sister is someone she wishes to protect." He rubbed his chin. "And a couple of servants."

Conn moved closer to his brother. "I know you'll not like it, but I'll offer this. Graeme, there appears to be something between you two. Why not marry her when this is over? Her husband will be gone, ye say she hates him, so she'll not be missing him. Ye can bring her daughter here and raise the bairn as your own. If ye want to take the lass to wife, do as she asks and save those who are close to her. They did not kill our parents. Ye have to settle with the Merrill and his warriors. I say we only kill those who try to stop our intent."

"I'll think on what ye say, but ye know the clan wants more. Our warriors want more."

"Aye, they do. Ye may convince them to spare Catherine's life, especially if ye plan to take her as your wife. They would even agree to sparing the wee lassie, but they'll want his mother or his sister for Mama's life, and the son for Alpin. But if ye do that, ye may ruin your chances with Catherine. Killing a wee lad or anyone she loves will not help a relationship."

"I agree, but how could I convince them that justice is served by taking Merrill and his warriors only?" This is what he wanted to do, but he knew his clan would expect the Merrill's heir to be killed.

"Take Catherine back, have her spy as evidence that she is on our side. The more attached our clan becomes to her, the more we can convince them of what she wishes. After all, she could be our mistress. If ye spare many, the MacGregor clan could benefit. We could take more into our clan, make our castle vibrant again. Finish this and accept any willing to swear fealty. 'Tis the right thing to do. If we can get on with our lives, mayhap so Boyd can move on, too."

Graeme peered at his brother, uncertain of how he should respond. "I'll think on it. I have a few days. We shall see what information Catherine gives us. I know not whether I can trust her yet."

Shouts from the front gates interrupted their conversation. Graeme jerked his head back to look over his land.

Four men in Merrill colors headed toward their gates. *How dare they…*

Without thinking, he rushed to the door and ran down the staircase, Conn yelling behind him, "Graeme, we must finish this later. Do no' be rash. We can continue as we've planned, just hide the lass here."

Graeme did not acknowledge his brother's words. The Merrills were on *his* land. He tore down the rest of the steps, then raced out of the great hall faster than he'd ever run before. His hand traveled to his claymore sheathed at his side, and he felt something come to life inside him. This was not just blind rage; this was more.

Charging toward the stables, Graeme bellowed orders to his men along the way, Conn following directly behind him. The lads had already saddled his horse, so he leaped atop Starlight and galloped through the gate his guards had opened for him, pleased to the see the flurry of activity as his warriors followed his lead.

Once outside the gates, he stared at the four men gathered in front of him. None of them were Henry Merrill.

"State your business or die at my sword," Graeme yelled.

The one in the front shouted, "We are searching for the Merrill's wife."

The warrior next to him said, "His wife cuckolded him,

and we're here to see she gets her just reward for it."

The third one said, "And not just with one man. Merrill just discovered his wife is a whore. She has been warming many beds, and we have his permission to use her freely, if you get my meaning." He grinned and his eyes lit up. "She is a beauty. Mayhap if you're nice to us, we'll allow you a taste after we're all done with her."

Graeme saw red.

Catherine paced inside the MacGregor's chamber, reviewing everything he'd said to her. Though she still hobbled and winced in pain, pacing helped her work through everything in her mind. Whenever Henry locked her in a chamber, this was her first reaction. She would pace and pace to calm the fear in her blood, the fear of what would come next from her husband.

This was different. She did not fear Graeme MacGregor. While she did not doubt he would kill her husband when he found the chance, she knew he'd never hurt her. Despite all his bluster and hard edge, she could not imagine him hurting innocents. After seeing him with his brothers, she believed he carried a deeper goodness hidden behind the coldness in his eyes. She wasn't sure how she knew, but she did. She would do what she could to uncover this part of him, though she could not explain why.

It was something she had to do. Graeme MacGregor was a mystery to her, but also a challenge.

She stopped pacing and moved over to Graeme's bed, lying down and resting her head on a soft pillow that carried his scent. She breathed in deeply, trying to identify each component, and finally decided it was a mixture of pine and soap and mint. It smelled just as he did when he stood close to her.

She rubbed her fingers across her lips, the lips he'd kissed, thinking about how he'd taught her a wee bit about the tenderness that could exist between a man and a woman.

She wondered what it would be like to start a life with Graeme MacGregor. Her marital duties had always been something she both dreaded and hated. Painful, though quick. She imagined it would not be painful with Graeme—he would not allow it to be painful.

She would like to know what that felt like.

Her eyes widened at the path her thoughts had taken. How she wished things were different. The opportunity to leave her cruel husband was here, yet her daughter was still under his power, and she could never leave Issy. Truth was, if she had to choose freedom or her daughter, she'd choose her daughter. She'd already been gone too long, though injury prevented it from being any other way. As soon as she was able, she'd return, with or without Graeme's help.

Loud noises from below jolted her to attention. She hurried over to the door, but it was impossible to determine the source of the sudden chaos. She opened the door just a crack, pleased to see Rory hadn't locked her inside. People were running everywhere, yelling to each other, but she was too far away to understand any of it.

They all headed out the door. Once the great hall was empty, she crept down the staircase and over to the door, opening it just a touch in the hopes that voices and sounds would drift out to her.

She heard the pounding of horses' hooves moving away from her. Suddenly frightened of what could be happening, she wiped the sweat from her palms down the gown she wore. Could this mean that her husband's men had arrived? If so, she wished to hear what they said, wished to see if her husband was here with them.

Chewing her lip, she thought about what to do next, but she was certain of one thing. Even though Graeme had made her promise to stay inside, she could not allow him or his men to be endangered because of her—not after all they'd already suffered from Henry.

The sounds drifted farther away from her, so she opened the door to see where everyone had gone, the heavy oak almost knocking her over. The courtyard was empty. Puzzled, she scanned the area until she found the bulk of the MacGregor warriors. The gates were open and they were outside on horseback.

She did what her gut told her to do. Cursing the boar for injuring her, she did her best to get down the staircase without causing herself further injury. Fortunately, she was able to limp to the gate without anyone questioning her. Graeme's voice carried over the distance, but she was unable to hear his words.

She managed to find a hiding spot just over the bridge and off to the side of the gate—a vantage point that would allow her to focus on her husband's men. What she heard shocked her.

"We are searching for the Merrill's wife."

The warrior next to the man who'd spoken said, "His wife cuckolded him, and we're here to see she gets her just reward for it."

The third one chuckled and said, "And not just with one man. Merrill just discovered his wife is a whore. She has been warming many beds, and we have his permission to use her freely, if you get my meaning." She was close enough to see his sick grin. "She is a beauty. Mayhap if you're nice to us, we'll allow you a taste after we're all done with her."

Catherine's eyes widened and her jaw fell open. How

could they say such a thing about her? Forgetting about what Graeme had told her, she plowed her way through the crowd, pushing men aside so she could hobble through to where the horses faced off.

She could not see Graeme's face, but he never moved, his hand resting on the hilt of his claymore.

Something inside Catherine snapped. All the atrocities she'd been forced to endure suddenly burst inside her head, stealing all of her reason. She shrieked and stumbled forward, swinging her fist at her husband's men. "Lies! You tell lies about me. 'Tis not true! None of it."

Graeme turned in time to catch her heading toward the horses.

"Catherine, get back!"

But she kept on, unable to stop herself.

CHAPTER SEVEN

F EAR GRIPPED GRAEME AS HE watched Catherine run into the middle of the gathering of horses, screaming at her husband's men. One of them reached for her and yanked on her hair, pulling her back toward him.

Graeme lost his ability to reason. He kneed his horse and pulled out his claymore, swinging it over his head. For fear he would hurt Catherine, he swung the flat of the blade toward the men rather than the edge.

The fools were all staring at Catherine, so they didn't see him coming until he was upon them. The first went flying off his horse, then the second, the third, and the fourth. He jumped off his horse and yelled at Catherine, "Move, Catherine. Take yourself away."

She spun in a circle as the horses around her shuffled in confusion, some rearing up on their hind legs. Covering her head, she tottered away at the same time Graeme shoved her behind him before he went after her husband's men.

He stuck his blade in the belly of the man who'd dared to touch her hair, then roared with satisfaction as he went after the second one coming directly at him. He took his stance and sliced from the side, knocking the fool's weapon from his hands and carving him across the chest, blood spurting everywhere.

He continued as if possessed, never losing focus, intent on killing all of them for daring to say such things about Catherine. Despite the logical, calm way he'd discussed his options with Conn, his gut told him she was his, not Merrill's. Other guards moved in to assist him, but he yelled, "Leave me. They are mine."

He swung his weapon over his head, bringing it down on the third guard, who'd turned his attention to Catherine. He killed him with one swoop of his blade, then chased after the last warrior, his sword whistling through the air before it plunged into his belly. The man fell and Graeme yanked his blade out before cleaning it on the man's Merrill plaid.

He stood and looked over the four men he'd just killed, panting with the exertion it had required to take four men down. A voice yelled from behind—his brother's—but he ignored him. Instead, he mounted his horse and headed straight for Catherine, who was now screaming with her hands over her head, doing her best to race across the meadow.

Looking down from his stallion, he said to his guards, "Do not follow me. I do this alone." He gave Conn a nod and took off after her, coming upon her quickly and scooping her up from behind. The relief he felt when he lowered her sideways into his lap told him how much this woman had already changed him.

She let out another gut-wrenching squeal, followed by a sob that came from deep within her, and he slowed his horse so he could put one hand to her cheek and force her to look at him.

"Catherine, 'tis me, Graeme. I'll not hurt you."

She still held a crazed look in her eyes, but he was

determined to reach her. This lass was *strong*. He'd never seen another woman take on four men on horseback for telling lies about her. "Catherine, look at me. They are gone, they'll not touch ye ever again. I told ye I would protect you."

Her breath hitched and she continued to sob, but her hand finally came up to his cheek as she stared at him. "Graeme?"

"Aye. I've got ye. I'll not allow anything to happen to you…ever." He kissed her forehead and led his horse into the forest, slowing to a trot to make sure they stayed on the path.

"Graeme," she closed her eyes. "They were lies, all lies, I never…"

He stopped his horse and wrapped one arm around her, taking hold of her chin with the other hand. "I know. They were lies meant to goad me."

"But…but…"

"Hush. 'Tis all fine now." He kissed her cheek then kissed her lightly on the lips.

"Graeme?"

"Aye?" He kissed one corner of her mouth and then the other, doing his best to calm her. His cock had sprung to life as soon as he'd wrapped his arms around her, the fury of the battle still fresh in his blood.

"Love me, Graeme. Please? I want to know what it should be like. I need to know."

He growled and tugged her close, kissing her lips with a roughness that frightened even him, but she clung to him, returning his fervor with everything she had. Running his hands down her back and up her front, he paused to cup her breasts. Then he slid the garment off her shoulders, opening her beauty to him.

He moaned and took her nipple in his mouth while she

arched against him, pushing and gripping his arms. When he was able to pull himself away from her luscious curves, he lifted her from his lap and set her down on the ground, sliding off his horse next to her.

He carried her into a small clearing covered with soft moss. He set her down, then removed his plaid and tunic and tossed it onto the ground before helping her disrobe. When they were finally settled on his plaid, he balanced himself on his elbows and said, "Are you sure ye want this?"

"Aye. I do, but I know not what to do. Ye must show me." She glanced at him with innocent eyes and whispered, "Do you want this?"

He grinned and glanced down at his erection. "Need ye ask that question, lass? There's nothing I want more at this moment. I have wanted ye since the moment I saw you. But ye are so beautiful that once I start, I may not be able to stop myself. 'Tis why I ask you if ye are sure."

She nodded and he kissed her, a deep kiss to tell her how much he wanted her. He was not much with words, instead running his hands all over her soft skin, hoping to pleasure her.

He caressed her and trailed kisses across her porcelain skin, delighting in her taste and her scent. Once his hands traveled below and he opened her, delving into her slit with his fingers, he was pleased to find that she wanted him as much as he did her. Poised over her, he told himself to go slowly, but he could not, instead thrusting inside her with a grunt of pleasure.

He roared to life and picked up his rhythm, though she did not move with him. She glanced at him in confusion, and he whispered, "Come with me." But he suspected she had no idea of what he spoke.

"Tell me what ye like, sweet one. I'll bring ye to your

peak with me." The expression on her face told him her husband had been a selfish brute.

Catherine did not care that Graeme was not her husband. She wanted him because she wished to feel loved, to feel special, just to *feel*. Because the expression in his gaze, on his face, told her he believed she was beautiful. She would allow him to do whatever he wished with her, no matter how much it hurt. He'd just killed four men for her honor.

She stared into his eyes when he entered her—and was shocked to realize that it did not hurt at all.

In fact, she wished for more. In the past, she'd often counted, staring at the ceiling until her husband finished with a grunt and removed himself. But this was different. Without being aware of it, she grasped Graeme's hips and tried to pull him closer. She had a sudden need for all of him inside her, and she did not wish to be slow about it.

He whispered to her as he moved inside of her, asking her what she liked, what she wanted. She had no notion of what he meant, but she said, "More. Faster. I dinnae know."

He picked up his rhythm and she lost the ability to think, following his lead and moving with him. He reached down between them and touched a spot that made her squeal and squirm, but she wanted him to continue, so she spread her legs wider to give him better access.

He caressed the spot until something came over her, a darkness that turned bright, and she called out to him, not understanding what was happening but reveling in it. She gripped his arms as she tipped over the edge into pleasure. He must have done the same because he yelled and growled, holding her as if he would never let her go, as if she had given him a gift that she didn't comprehend.

When he finished, he kissed her and asked, "Did I hurt you?"

"Nay." She stared at him, lost in his blue gaze. He started to pull away from her, but she clenched her muscles. "Nay, do not leave me yet. Please?" She wanted to remember this moment forever. Graeme made her feel like a woman, and more important, he made her feel wanted—a sensation she never wished to forget.

He grinned and said, "All right. Can ye roll with me? I fear I'm too heavy for you."

He rolled onto his back and brought her with him, not breaking their connection. "Though I will fall out soon."

"Ye will?"

"Aye, I'm shrinking."

"Oh. I hadnae noticed." She rested her head on his chest, listening to his strong heartbeat. "I dinnae want it to end yet."

He wrapped his arms around her and she huddled into his warmth, not caring that she was unclothed before him. This had been the most beautiful experience of her life.

"My guess is ye havenae enjoyed mating with your husband."

She picked her head up to peer at him. "Never. 'Tis no' the same thing at all. With you, 'tis something special. With my husband, I hated it." She lay her head back down on his chest. "My thanks for protecting me against my husband's men."

He sighed, caressing her back with one hand and then running his fingers through the strands of her hair. "I should be angry with ye for disobeying me and running outside, but I cannae, because if ye had not, we would not be here on this soft moss, and I will treasure this memory. I dinnae have many moments like this in my life."

She closed her eyes, wishing she could stay in his arms forever.

"My sweet, I fear we will be found out if I dinnae get ye dressed and return ye to my keep."

She startled, realizing he was being truthful with her. She did not wish to be found in such a state, even if it was only by his brothers.

They both stood, and he grabbed her gown and his plaid and took her over to the small burn running between the trees. He washed her with a linen square he'd pulled from his sporran before helping her with her shift and her gown. She did her best to run her fingers through her wild hair, but he stopped her. "Do no'. I love your hair. 'Tis a glorious shade, and I like to see it down and wild."

She blushed and stopped her fussing. "Thank ye."

When they finished, he helped her onto his horse and mounted behind her, pulling her close as they trotted back toward his keep.

Regardless of anything else that happened, she would never forget this moment with him. She would treasure it always.

CHAPTER EIGHT

I T WAS NEARLY DARK WHEN they returned. Graeme did not rush his horse simply because he felt a new, unfamiliar peace inside. Aye, he'd enjoyed women before, but not like this…

He would kill Henry Merrill and most of his warriors. Where would Catherine go? His mind moved in directions it had never gone before. Once he finished this and vengeance was theirs, why could he not marry and have a chance at happiness?

Happiness. Something he hadn't experienced in a long, long time. Perhaps Conn's advice was worth considering.

But would Catherine truly marry her husband's killer?

When they arrived back outside the gates, he was pleased to see his second had already arranged for the bodies to be buried off in the distance. Normally, he would not go to the trouble of burying enemies, but circumstances were such that he would do well to hide their deaths until they were ready to attack.

Conn and Rory followed them to the stables, and Conn helped Catherine dismount. Rory's excitement was enough for ten people.

"Graeme, ye fought like a possessed animal. Ye took on

four men, killing them all. Everyone says ye must be the best warrior in all the land."

The lad was practically jumping up and down as he said it. His excitement was infectious, and several men yelled their congratulations to Graeme as they made their way through the courtyard. Graeme clasped his brother's shoulder, keeping his other hand at the small of Catherine's back. Conn gave him a pointed look, but he just smiled and moved closer to Catherine.

Rory stopped in his tracks. "Graeme? Ye just smiled." He glanced at Conn and Catherine for confirmation.

"Aye, he did," Conn added. "I saw it, too, Rory. Mayhap once this is over, our clan can smile a bit more often."

Inside the hall, Graeme led Catherine to a chair in front of the hearth and built up the fire. Summer nights could be cool in the Highlands, and he did not want her to catch a chill. Moyra bustled up, and he gave her instructions for the evening. "Moyra, Catherine has had a difficult day, so please settle her in my chamber, and send a platter of food and a tub bath for her."

Catherine peeked over her shoulder at him, a confused expression on her face, though he did not understand why. She'd been in his chamber last night.

"She's sleeping with you?" Rory asked, his eyes wide.

Graeme weighed his words carefully before he spoke, wishing to give Catherine the respect she deserved. "Aye, 'tis where she is safest. Catherine will sleep in my bed, and I will sleep on the floor. I expect the Merrills will pay us another visit once their laird discovers he's lost four of his men. I couldnae sleep if I had to worry about her in a chamber alone. 'Tis my job to protect her, as ye know, Rory."

"They were telling lies about ye, were they no', my lady?" Rory asked.

"Aye, they were all lies," Graeme grumbled. "How could ye think otherwise of her? They wished to make me angry so I would lose control."

Rory's eyes lit up again. "But they dinnae, did they, my laird? All of the Scots will be talking about ye soon after a fight like that. You'll be a hero."

"Except we dinnae want the word spread about the Merrill's men for a while yet. We shall not travel off our land until I plan our next step."

"Do ye think the Merrill himself will come here?" Rory asked.

"Nay, but he'll send more men, probably on the morrow or the next day. 'Tis why I must protect Catherine the best way I know how. She'll not leave my side."

Moyra had left to do the laird's bidding, but now returned to the hearth. She nodded to Graeme. "Your chamber is ready for her. I gave her the best linens we have, my laird."

Catherine followed Moyra up the stairs, but not before glancing over her shoulder at Graeme, something that pleased him immensely. As soon as the women were out of earshot, Conn asked, "What's your plan? Do we go after him on the morrow?"

Graeme's gaze followed Catherine as she mounted the steps, sweet memories washing over him. "Nay. I may send someone back for more information, but we willnae travel there yet. I agree with Tomag. Too many of his warriors are out searching for Catherine, and now they will be searching for four guards. When we attack their land, I wish to be certain Merrill is there. It would be disastrous to strike while he's away from home."

"We wait." He sighed as he watched her sashaying hips move toward the door to his chamber.

He threw the rest of his ale down and headed toward

the door.

"Where are ye goin' now?" Rory asked.

"To the loch for a bath. I need to think. Ye may join me if ye can be quiet." He glanced over his shoulder at his youngest brother. The lad hated bathing and avoided it as much as possible.

Rory shook his head vehemently. "Nay. I'll stay here and guard the lady."

"Conn and Tomag will guard Catherine. When was the last time ye bathed, Rory? The lady will not enjoy the odor ye send out if ye wait any longer."

Rory scowled and stared at the floor, a pout about to blossom.

"How long, Rory?" Graeme paused at the door.

"A long time." He hung his head, obviously hoping his brother would relent. They'd not had any women but Moyra to speak about their ways. Graeme often acted as sire to his younger brothers.

"Come. 'Tis warm enough for ye to enjoy the loch." He held the door and nodded to Rory who finally slunk forward in his direction, his shoulders slumped.

As soon as they arrived at the loch, Graeme dropped his garments and ran toward the water. He knew the exact spot where it was deepest and dove in headfirst. Rory followed. Once they both surfaced, Graeme asked his brother, "Why must I beg ye to come here? The loch is refreshing in early summer. Do ye no' remember the times when the five of us would swim together, splashing each other while Papa swam across the loch?"

Rory shook his head. "I dinnae recall much of Alpin."

Graeme rolled onto his back, floating. "That is most unfortunate. It saddens me. But ye were only four summers, the same age as Catherine's daughter."

Rory tread water not far from him. "She has a daughter?"

"Aye." He stared up at the clouds, wondering what the wee lass looked like.

"Graeme, why do we no' have many women and bairns about?"

"Och, lad. I fear 'tis because I work our men too hard. I have plans for our clan once we finally put our revenge behind us. We could have festivities once a week with dancing and huge platters of food, outside in the summers and in the hall in the winter." He smiled as memories from the time before the slaughter washed over him. "I know what our men need—contests like the ones Papa used to have."

"What kind of contests, Graeme?"

"Papa's favorites were the contests of strength, but he also held contests to determine the best swordsman or the finest rider. He'd see who could bring down the biggest boar or deer. Who could find the biggest pheasant. Then we'd finish with tables and tables of roasted meat, meat pies, the best ales, even some wine. Mama loved wine."

"Truly?" He kicked his legs as he splashed about. "What else do ye recall?"

"Sometimes we would have vendor fairs, too, where people would barter for special items. The most popular booth carried ribbons. The warriors would tie them to the ends of their swords and the lasses would try to sweet talk them into a ribbon for their hair."

"Graeme, ye would have the most lasses after you. You'd have to barter many ribbons."

"Alpin gave ten away once, I recall." The thought made him grin. It had been a long time since he'd thought of the good memories of his family. What they'd been like before the Merrill had torn them apart. "The lasses would wear the ribbons woven into their hair," he continued.

"The more colors they had, the more they strutted around the courtyard."

"Catherine would have the most if she was not married."

He tousled the lad's hair. "We could celebrate the holidays again, something we have not done in seven years. Would ye like that?"

Rory moved to a spot shallow enough for him to stand, and he ducked under the water to grab rocks to skip across the surface. "Aye. All would be welcome to me. I wish things to be different. I dinnae remember Mama or Papa, only ye and Conn and Boyd. I wish we had more wives and young ones in our village."

"Ye havenae had many to play with, have ye, Rory? I seem to have failed ye there." Graeme swam toward his brother, who now stood at the water's edge with handful of stones, shaking the drops from his hair and his body. "Boyd isnae capable of playing, is he? I keep hoping someday. I talk to him every day, hoping he will answer me, but he still hasn't."

Graeme clasped his brother's shoulder. "Dinnae despair. I suspect much will be changing in a short time. Now, do ye care to race me back?"

A short time later, they returned to the keep, both laughing. Rory whispered before they moved inside, "I like it when ye are happy, Graeme. 'Tis the lady who makes ye smile?"

Graeme didn't know how to answer him, other than to be truthful. There was no sense denying what was now obvious to everyone around them. "Aye. I dinnae understand it, but Catherine makes me smile."

When they stepped inside, the hall was almost empty. "I like her, too," Rory whispered.

Graeme clasped his shoulder, but then gave him a light

shove toward the staircase. "Off with ye, lad. There is much to do on the morrow."

He grabbed an ale and moved to the hearth, staring into the dying flames and the embers. He ran his hand down his face. Aye, Catherine made him smile, more than he'd like to admit. She'd bewitched him for sure. What was he to do about it?

She could be with child, but he'd not know for some time. If she carried his bairn, he wished to know. If he could, he'd lock her in the tower room and keep her forever. But he knew he could not. She would ask to return to her daughter soon. The love for her child was evident in everything she said, and he could see it in her eyes. How he wished he saw the same love for *him* in those haunting green orbs.

He fell into a chair and leaned forward, elbows resting on his knees.

Catherine was dangerous. She distracted him from his purpose, and though she was the most delightful distraction he'd ever known, she was still a distraction.

He knew it would make sense to bring her back to her husband, as he'd mentioned to Conn. If he brought her back, she could draw a map of the inside of the castle for him. That was the only information missing, the last piece he needed to plan his attack. They could succeed without it, he was sure, but with it, they'd be invincible.

Traveling with her would give him the chance to assess the castle himself up close. He'd take a score of warriors to protect her…yet he knew he could not do it. He could not hand her over to the cruel bastard, even if he was her husband.

Not after what they'd just shared.

Everything had changed.

Catherine kneaded her hands in her lap as she stared at the roaring fire in the hearth in front of her. What would happen this night? Would Graeme be in her bed?

Moyra had helped her bathe and given her a beautiful night rail to wear, one she tugged tight around her, feeling a chill in the air though she sat a short distance from the fire. She'd glanced over her shoulder three times already, hoping the door would open and he would fill the doorway and step inside.

Graeme MacGregor confused her like no other. He was the only man she'd ever trusted besides her loyal manservant, Benneit. Graeme had shown her things she did not know existed—tenderness, gentleness, soft caresses, and the sharing of pleasure.

But this happiness was not hers to keep. She'd ask him to take her back to her sweet Issy on the morrow. She brushed a tear away that had sat in the corner of her eye for several minutes.

She'd been away from her daughter for too long. Who knew when Graeme would attack? If he did not go for her husband for a sennight, her dear Issy could be dead by then. Guilt washed over her at the thought of how long she'd already been away.

Besides, Margaret and Wesley could still be in danger.

Her mind was in such turmoil, she knew not where to go or what to do. Perhaps she'd wait until the morrow to make her decision. She'd not return in the dark. That was frightening enough for her. When she returned, it would be during daylight. Aye, she'd go back, but she could see no reason why she could not enjoy this night as much as possible first.

She wanted Graeme, wished to touch him again, to

bring him pleasure, and to relax in the warmth of his arms. There she felt safe and secure, protected from the cruel men of the world, mostly her own husband.

Lying in Graeme MacGregor's arms was the best place to be in the land.

The door opened, and Graeme finally stepped inside, just as she had hoped, closing the door behind him and bolting it. She jumped out of her chair and turned to face him, her back to the fire. He leaned against the door and smiled. His hair was still damp, curled at his shoulders, and saints above, he was the most handsome man she'd ever seen in her short life. Why, she swore if she lived a dozen lives, she'd never see a man as attractive as Graeme MacGregor.

He smiled. "Catherine, ye are a most pleasing sight to me, sweeter than the most beautiful flower in any meadow. The flames behind you show me every curve of your body." He pushed away from the door and grabbed a pillow and a blanket from a chest, tossing them onto the floor in front of the door. He removed his sword and set it down on the same chest.

She scratched her head and stumbled for her words, starting several times before she was confident enough to speak. "Graeme, ye will sleep on the floor?"

He removed his plaid and stood in only his tunic, his hands on his hips. "Aye, sweet Catherine. This time, if ye want me, ye must invite me to your bed. I'll not force myself on ye ever."

"Ye did not force yourself on me. I was willing."

"Aye, 'tis true, but the emotions of the battle have left us. Now we can act with reason."

"Do ye not want to be in my bed?"

He took two slow steps until he stood directly in front of her. Lifting her chin so he could gaze into her eyes, he said, "Och, there is nothing that would please me more, but my honor tells me that this time, ye must invite me. And as for wanting ye?" He glanced down at his growing erection pressing against his hose. "I think ye know the answer to that."

She swallowed as she glanced down his body, then brought her gaze back up to meet his. She reached for the ribbon that held the front of her gown together, pulled on it and slid the night rail off her shoulders until it fell to the floor. It was her way of telling him what she wanted. Once she stood bare to him, she whispered, "Would ye come to my bed, Graeme?"

He removed his tunic and then drew her mouth to his, nipping at her bottom lip and running his tongue across the length of it. "Catherine, ye could make a sane man daft. Aye, nothing would please me more than to warm ye in my bed."

She sighed and fell against him, parting her lips for him. He kissed her, this time with such tenderness she could not stop the moan from deep within her belly. She tasted the mint leaves he had been chewing and the ale he'd probably just had. This man was the most delectable thing she'd ever tasted. She lost her balance when he bent to kiss a trail down her shoulder and over her chest, but he caught her. He kissed a complete circle around each breast before touching the tip of his tongue to her nipple. She jerked in response, her body filling with sensations she could not control, already taut with need for this man.

He chuckled and moved down her body, dropping to his knees in front of her, kissing her belly and her hips. "Ye are a siren of sheer beauty, and I must have all of you." He placed several kisses down each hip and over to the vee in her legs, kissing her there, in a place she had never expected. Her hands threaded through his hair, clinging to him as he brought his tongue back to that certain spot, setting her need afire and causing her knees to buckle under her.

He laughed and stood, lifting her into his arms and whispering, "My Catherine, ye are a passionate one, are ye no'? Aye, but 'tis true ye please me, woman."

He settled her in bed, gazing upon her before he climbed in and rolled onto his side next to her, his fingers weaving a scintillating path of pleasure all over her body. "This time, we shall do it slowly."

And they did. Graeme MacGregor brought her into a world she'd never known before. With every kiss he feathered onto her body, her breath caught; with every touch, she ached. He could bring her body to sensual peaks that made her forget her own name, until she finally crashed over the edge of ecstasy.

She enjoyed watching Graeme's pleasure as much as her own. After she screamed his name and he whispered hers, he hugged her close, not letting go of her until their breathing slowed. She had a sudden need to know everything about him, learn all about his body, his clan, his heritage.

Graeme rolled onto his back and tugged her next to him, tucking her under his arm so her head rested on his shoulder. "Did I please ye?"

"Aye. 'Twas sweeter than the first time."

He chuckled and kissed her forehead. "Tell me how ye ended up with the Merrill. Who is your sire?"

His question caught her off guard—he wanted to know about her as she did him. She twirled her finger in the dark hairs on his chest to keep from showing him the emotion in her eyes. "My sire is Clyde Beaton. I have two brothers, Edwin and Edward, and one sister younger than me, Anna. My father sold me to the Merrill for a bag of gold coins."

"Did he not know what kind of man he was?"

Memories flooded her mind—her father hitting her mother, ordering her about, telling her not to speak, ridiculing her whenever it suited him. He'd rarely spoken to his daughters, which had suited Catherine fine. Her mother almost never stood up to him, which broke Catherine's heart. The one time she had tried to stand up for her mother, he'd backhanded her hard enough to knock her to the floor.

After that, her mother had begged her not to intervene. She hadn't understood her mother's motivations at the time, but she did now. A mother's love was a fierce emotion. Catherine also understood how being married to a cruel man could break a person and how the abuse could weaken your defenses, your will to fight.

She had promised herself she would never stop fighting for her own daughter.

"I doubt he knew much about the Merrill. It would not matter to my sire. He hit my mother often, so I was not surprised when Henry first slapped me. I thought it was the way for every marriage."

She leaned up on one elbow to gaze at him. "Why are ye different? Many men slap their wives in my sire's clan, though few of them inflict the kinds of punishments Henry favors. I was always told it was how a man made his wife obey him, but ye have shown me something different."

He ran his finger down her jawline and across her bottom lip. "My sire never hit my mother. He taught me and my brothers to respect women. Since they are not the same size, 'tis not a fair fight in my eyes. I cannae see it any other way."

She brought his finger into her mouth and sucked on it

for a quick moment, wanting more of him. "And I appreciate ye for that. It makes ye more of a man in my eyes."

"I am not afraid of a woman. I would allow ye to have power over me."

"How would ye do that?" she asked, more than slightly curious.

His blue eyes turned dark, a look she was starting to recognize.

"I'd be pleased to show ye." His smirk told her it had something to do with coupling. "Ye may do it however ye'd like. I'll let ye decide."

"I dinnae understand," she whispered.

"Bring this leg over me, and I'll teach ye."

She straddled him, feeling his erection growing underneath her, making her want to rub against him.

"Go ahead, lass. Do whatever ye'd like to please yourself. I'm at your mercy." He placed his hands behind his head and grinned.

She sat up straight and settled her hands on his chest, then decided to play with his body the way he had played with hers. Starting with his nipples, she rubbed each one with her fingers before bending over to use her tongue on the taut peaks, even grazing her teeth over one. He groaned and she sat back up, watching him.

"Do no' stop."

She pushed herself up on her knees, then reached down to take his erection in her hand, circling it with her palm, and then rubbed the tip against her pleasure point, surprising herself with a moan when she found the right spot.

"Here, allow me to help." He set his thumb to caressing her in the same place, and her hands fell back to brace herself on his thighs.

She allowed him to continue this until she could stand

it no longer, then reached down to guide him inside her. "I love to feel ye inside me, Graeme. Ye fill me perfectly."

His hands moved up to massage her breasts, and she started to move on him, her rhythm increasing. "Do ye like being in control, Catherine?"

All she could do was nod, her need picking up and forcing her to lower herself over Graeme to manage the pace she wanted. He gripped her hips, and she brought him in and out, thrusting him inside her as far as she could. She whimpered until her orgasm crashed over her, and he came at the exact same time.

When she was sure they were both finished, she fell on him, her breathing raspy. "I like it any way ye like it, Graeme."

Graeme made love to her two more times in the night, and she could do nothing but cling to him and weep each time she peaked from his lovemaking.

She wished the night could go on forever.

When he awakened the next morning, he turned his head and smiled as soon as he saw Catherine. Still asleep, she was a beauty all tousled. While he'd love nothing more than to awaken her, he'd kept her up enough last night and decided to allow her to sleep.

He climbed out of bed and donned his plaid—all he needed to wear to the hall. He'd just thrown the length over his shoulder when a knock came at his door. He opened it to peek out, not wanting anyone to see the lovely lass in his bed.

Rory stood there wide-eyed. "Come quickly. 'Tis Boyd."

He ran his hand though his hair, hoping Catherine's visit had not been too much for the lad. If he had retreated further into himself, Graeme did not know if he could handle it. It was far too painful to see what the Merrill's actions had done to Boyd. He said a quick prayer that he would find Boyd the same and no worse. "I'll meet ye down in the hall, Rory. Give me a moment."

Rory took off down the passageway. Graeme turned around to see a pair of green eyes staring at him, Catherine's mind clearly still cloudy as she rubbed the sleep from her face. He leaned over the bed and kissed her. "Go back to sleep, 'tis only Boyd."

"May I come with you?"

"That may not be wise. Boyd has only spoken to me for the past year. Mayhap seeing ye was too much for him."

She stared into his eyes for a moment, then surprised him by saying, "Please take me with ye? I'd like to see him again. If he does not want me, I'll leave. I'll take just a moment."

He took a deep breath before he answered. Protecting Boyd from further trauma was foremost in his mind, but a part of him thought Catherine had been good for Boyd. He'd smiled at her, a rare occurrence. Thoughts of Rory and what he'd said about wishing there were more women around the clan came rushing back to him. Could it be possible that Boyd felt the same? Moyra was much like a mother to him, but Catherine was different—warm, gracious, and comforting. Mayhap the lad saw her as a source of comfort, something he was lacking in his secluded life.

"I'll take you along, but if he seems at all upset, you'll have to go."

She nodded and bolted out of bed. She did her best to straighten her hair, while Graeme did his best not to laugh at her flimsy efforts. There was no fixing that wild mass of curls.

"Come to the hall. I'll wait for ye there. Give ye some privacy." He opened the door and cast a quick glance back at her before he closed it. She was a sight that could set everything right in his world. A stunning beauty, capable of both innocence and feistiness. He was unsure which quality he preferred.

Rory was waiting for him at a trestle table in the great hall, and Graeme sat opposite him, motioning to a serving girl to get him some porridge. "What is it this time, Rory?"

"He wanted me to get you."

Graeme stopped his hand in midair, deciding he couldn't straighten his hair any more than Catherine could fix hers. "What? How did ye know that? Did he speak my name?"

"Nay. He was agitated and restless, and Moyra kept guessing. When she said your name, he nodded."

This was a new development. "He nodded? For certes?" True, his brother had readily spoken with him and Catherine, but to his knowledge, Boyd had never answered Moyra.

"Aye. Moyra said 'twas pronounced. He wants you." Rory grabbed his hand to tug on it. "Can ye not come now?"

"Nay. I told Catherine I'd wait for her. She wishes to meet him." He would not tell Rory that he and Catherine had already been in to talk to him. He wouldn't risk hurting Rory's feelings any more than he would Boyd's.

"You'll take Catherine to meet Boyd? Why? Ye dinnae allow any others to see him."

"Catherine's different." He did not wish to examine why he had made that statement, and though he expected Rory would ask him to explain it, he was saved by Catherine making her way down the staircase.

He knew because every person in the hall stopped to gaze at her. She carried herself like a royal princess. He stood, and was pleased to see Rory rush forward to greet her.

"Good morn to ye, Catherine," his brother said.

"Good morn." She blushed, and Graeme hoped she was not embarrassed about sleeping in his chamber.

If he had his way, she'd never leave it.

"Would ye like some porridge?" Graeme asked, gesturing to the bowl the serving lass had just set down in front of him.

She shook her head. "Nay. I'll eat later."

"Good," Rory said. "Come along. We'll bring ye to Boyd's chamber."

Graeme rolled his eyes at Rory. The lad would never be able to wait for him to eat his porridge, so he abandoned it on the table and held his hand out to Catherine. She took it, a small smile on her face, and they followed Rory back up the stairs and down the passageway to Boyd's chamber.

As soon as they entered the room, Rory hurried to his elder brother's bedside. Boyd was now ten and four, yet he had none of the musculature of his brothers, nor was his skin bronzed from the sun. Pale, quiet, timid—three qualities that made Graeme wish to choke the life from the Merrill with his bare hands every time he visited with his brother.

"Boyd, this is Catherine. I found her in the forest, being chased by a boar." He thought it best to hide their previous interaction from Rory, and he suspected Boyd wouldn't say or do anything to indicate he'd already met Catherine.

To his shock, Boyd turned his head and smiled at Catherine.

Boyd *rarely* smiled.

Rory bounced from one foot to the other. "Ye like Catherine? She's nice, Boyd."

Graeme grabbed Boyd's hand and asked, "Did ye wish

to see me?"

Boyd nodded and opened his mouth to speak…nothing came out. Catherine, to Graeme's surprise, took the lad's wasted hand and cocooned it in hers. "Take all the time ye need, Boyd. We are in no hurry."

Boyd glanced at Graeme and attempted to speak again, but he still did not manage any words. Tears sprang to his eyes when he tried a third time with no success. Catherine said, "We'll come back another time, and ye can tell us then. Do not fret. I have a difficult time speaking early in the morn, too."

Graeme clasped his brother's shoulder and whispered, "Go ahead, Boyd. Rory misses ye as much as I do, and I'm sure Catherine would love to hear ye speak."

They gave him a few more moments, but when he didn't speak, Graeme placed his hand on Catherine's back and ushered her toward the door. He could not stand and watch the pain in his brother's face. At least he'd seen Boyd smile.

Rory said, "I'll stay on a wee bit and see if he speaks, Graeme."

"Aye. If ye need me again, come find me."

They were almost at the door, when Graeme was certain he heard a strangled sound. Could it have been Boyd's voice? He turned around and peered at his brother, Boyd's face red from exertion. His mouth opened again, and this time, the words rang out as loud as the clang of two swords in the lists.

"Kill Merrill, Graeme. Please?"

CHAPTER NINE

TWO DAYS LATER, GRAEME ENTERED the great hall much later than usual and Conn joined him shortly thereafter. He'd told Conn about Boyd's request, and they both felt the same way. Boyd would not heal until they had their revenge. He'd apologized to Catherine, but she claimed to understand.

Conn quirked his brow at his brother and gave him a knowing look. "Ye are late to rise. Are ye no' sleeping well?"

Graeme snorted. "I dinnae sleep much, but when I do, I sleep very well." He continued with his porridge, then broke off a chunk of the fresh bread in front of him. "Bread? Or are ye not eating?"

Conn shook his head as he looked down at his hands, playing with a stick he must have carried in from outside. So, he'd already been for a walk—a sure sign that Conn was buried deep in his thoughts. Finally, his brother said, "Do ye plan on marrying her when this is all over?"

Graeme set his food down and glared at his brother. "My only focus, at present, is revenge, just as it has always been. I'm giving protection to a woman who has been mistreated. 'Tis all ye need to concern yourself with at present."

"From what I hear, ye are giving her more than your protection."

Graeme shot off the bench so fast he knocked it over. He gripped his brother by the neck and whispered, "Be careful with your words. You'll not disrespect her. Do no' concern yourself with what goes on inside my chamber."

Conn's face turned red, but he managed to glower at his brother. "I fear 'tis almost impossible to ignore with the sounds that fill the halls in the dark of the night. I know I suggested marrying the lady, but I did not expect ye to treat her the way ye are."

Graeme set his brother down. "Ye need to focus on the Merrills. We will be attacking them soon."

Conn sat down at the table, rubbing his neck. "Are ye sure? Or are ye so besotted with the man's wife, you've given up on your life's goal?"

"I have not given up anything," he snarled. "The Merrill will still die at my hand, and I will also see to the death of any who stand in my way. Catherine has given me another good reason not to kill the women and children. Nothing else has changed."

His brother gave him a long look and then nodded. "If ye do not mind me speaking my thoughts, 'tis time to end it. We've waited long enough."

"Ye are correct, Conn. 'Tis time." He'd thought about all that he'd heard from Boyd, Conn, and Catherine. He would go after Merrill, his family, and his warriors. He hadn't settled on which members of his family he would spare, if any.

Conn's voice resounded in a tone he did not hear often. "Seeing ye with the lass is a reminder that we need to end this for our clan—seek our revenge and then get on with our lives. We are stagnant. We need women and bairns, laughter, and pride in our land. We've lost many, but we were too young to understand the importance of the women and married couples."

"I agree. The only promise I cannot make is the rest of his family. I have yet to make a decision about them. But ye are correct, we could use more additions to our clan." He'd had this same conversation with Rory not long ago, and he could not deny the last two days had been the best days he'd ever had with anyone. Perhaps, when this was done, they *could* marry. His brother was right. The time was here. "I agree with ye."

Tomag came in from outside and joined them.

"The men are working hard, practicing their sword arms?" Graeme asked, focusing on the food in front of him.

"Aye." He paused, then added, "Beg my pardon for speaking up, but ye promised an attack, and 'tis time to let them know your plans. If the lass has made ye change them, then I think 'tis only fair for our warriors to know."

Graeme nodded. "Conn and I were discussing the same."

"And your plan?" Tomag pressed.

He mulled over what he was to say to Tomag because he knew his men still wanted every member of Merrill's clan dead. He had decided not to kill everyone, and he'd not be swayed.

Graeme looked at Tomag. "Before I give my final decision, have ye heard any more about Merrill's men searching for his wife?"

"Nay. His men have not been seen. I worry that they have returned and are making plans, though I know not what. We must stay ahead of them," Tomag replied.

"I agree," Graeme said, stroking his chin. "We will attack soon, following our original plan."

Conn looked puzzled. "Have ye not put any more

thought to sending her back so she could spy on Merrill, then advise us of the castle's layout and his warriors?"

"Nay," he replied. "It would mean putting Catherine in danger, and I'll not do that. She drew me a map, but she does not know much. When we attack, we'll discover the layout, and I'll find her daughter in the keep. Catherine will know where she's kept. She's sickly and four summers old. How many others could there be?"

Tomag stood and paced in a circle, clearly disturbed about something.

"Speak your mind, Tomag."

He paced another circle, his hand shifting to the hilt of his sword and then off again, a gesture Graeme knew indicated he was upset.

"Seems I will." He stopped pacing and stood facing Graeme. "Ye've allowed your emotions to get involved. Ye were better off not caring about anyone in his keep at all. Now you'll hesitate. I say this because anyone who could look at this objectively would send Catherine back for more information, yet ye refuse. This action alone tells me ye are too involved."

Graeme stood, his hand moving to the hilt of his own sword. "Are ye suggesting that I'm an unfit leader? Do ye think I'll ever forgive the Merrill for killing my parents and my brother in front of me? For turning Boyd into a shadow of himself? Because if so, I'll tell ye that you are dead wrong." He started in a furious whisper and ended in a bellow.

Conn's head turned from one of them to the other, waiting to see what would happen next. Graeme was furious. His second's suggestion was traitorous.

Rather than back down, Tomag said, "I promised your sire to take care of ye lads. I made him that promise two days before his death, just as I had many times before.

Any time your sire had an inkling of trouble, I promised to watch over you. When he came to me that day, he was more concerned than usual. The Merrill had become irrational and daft, and the laird worried about his intentions. He hoped to avoid a confrontation, but as we all know, he could not."

He paused then added, "Ye have allowed a woman from another clan, one who was in bed with the devil a sennight ago, to turn your head."

Tomag's comment hit him square in the belly. He understood why the man was upset, but he could not allow his warriors to speak to him this way, especially not in the great hall for all to hear. "My goals are unchanged. Dinnae concern yourself with Catherine. I plan to keep her away from the Merrill's castle for a reason. We will attack the clan in two days and kill the Merrill and anyone who stands in our way. If ye think ye cannot fight for the MacGregor clan, then take yourself from our land."

Tomag paled, then nodded his head before staring at the ground. "My apologies, laird. I will inform your warriors that they must be ready to attack in two days. Is there anything else I can do to assist ye in this endeavor?"

"Aye, there is. Conn and I have made a decision and would like ye to prepare our warriors. We will not kill the women and children, but instead welcome any who wish to join our clan. Do ye think ye can convince our men that this is the righteous thing to do or do I need to speak to them?"

Tomag did his best to hide his grin. "Our warriors will support bringing women into the clan. Dinnae concern yourself with that. As long as the Merrill and his close family are dead, along with his warriors, they will accept it." Tomag stepped back and held his hand up. "I speak of Merrill family other than Catherine and her daughter.

And if I may be so bold, my laird?"

Graeme narrowed his gaze at his second. "Speak your mind."

"I'd be pleased to see a few more pretty faces here," he stared at the floor, the corner of his mouth twitching.

"Aye, I think we all would be pleased. Tell me more of why Papa suspected the Merrill would attack. What had happened? None of us know why Merrill killed our clanspeople in cold blood the way he did. Do ye know something we do not? Are ye hiding it? Conn and I deserve to know why."

Tomag shook his head, staring at his boots. "Your sire dinnae say, and 'twas no' my place to ask. I know no more than you." He paused for a moment, then asked again, "Anything else, my laird?"

"Nay, just ready our men. I'll join ye soon." He strode over to stand in front of his sire's invaluable second—a man who'd promised to serve him faithfully, as well. "I will see this through, Tomag. I promise ye." He clasped his shoulder.

Tomag met his gaze, and Graeme thought he saw moistness in the man's eyes. "My sincere apologies. I overstepped my bounds. What ye plan is right and just for what was done to you. 'Tis time for us to have our revenge at last."

Conn stood and added, "I agree, Tomag. We cannot forget our ultimate goal. While I understand Catherine's effect on you, it cannae change anything. This needs to be done, then ye and the lady may decide where ye go from here."

"Exactly," Graeme murmured.

Catherine closed the door as quietly as she could. She felt a wee bit of guilt for eavesdropping, but she needed to know Graeme's plans. He told her nothing, insisting that he would take care of everything and that he would bring Issy to her.

Except trusting a man was not so easy for her. After all the lies she'd been told by her husband and her father, all the abuses she'd suffered at their hands, she wondered how she could ever put her entire faith in any man.

Graeme had said he would attack in two days. He'd also said he was not sure if he would spare her husband's family.

She *had* to leave.

She had to know how her wee daughter fared, and besides, she felt a powerful need to protect Margaret, though she'd have to come up with a way to keep her from discovering the truth. Catherine had no warm feelings for Henry, but Margaret and Henry were blood relatives. Did she know of the tragedy her brother had orchestrated against the MacGregors?

With all she'd learned, her husband deserved what was planned for him, and his mother was just as nasty, self-serving, and cruel. But Margaret, Wesley, and Issy deserved none of what could happen to them. She'd come up with a strategy concerning Margaret later.

She trusted Graeme to keep his promise to save Issy, but if she didn't go to the castle with him, how would he even know where to find the lass? The drawings she'd made for him were from memory, and open to misinterpretation. What if he could not find her? Merrill's mother could run away with her, hide her somewhere, or even hurt her.

She could not take that chance. The only way she could ensure Issy was protected from the battle, and the fallout, would be to go to her. Another two days was too long to wait. Perhaps she could find Benneit and tell him to hide Issy, Margaret, and Wesley from the imminent attack. With any luck, she'd be able to do that in secret, without seeing Henry.

Standing with her back against the door, her mind raced with possibilities. What would she do? If she told Graeme her plans, he would lock her inside his castle for sure. She would have to steal a horse and find her way back.

Then another thought occurred to her…what would she do once she'd warned them? Henry would certainly find out she was there if she stayed very long. Should she run after speaking with Benneit? Find Issy, Margaret, and Wes and search for a cave for them to hide in? What lengths would she go to in order to protect Issy? Should she tell her husband to ensure the attack didn't happen at all?

Her shoulders slumped, and she fell into the nearest chair. Nay. She could not endanger Graeme any more than she could endanger Issy. In fact, leaving him would be the most difficult thing she'd ever done. She'd gone and lost her heart to him.

Perhaps she should speak to Graeme, find out more about his plans. Maybe she could even convince him to bring her to the Merrill keep.

Something told her it was paramount that she convince him to leave today. If he refused, she'd be forced to go alone. She grabbed her head, her mind suddenly hurting from all the choices and possibilities—what could go right and what could go wrong.

If she chose badly, she could lose everything.

The door opened and she spun around, pleased to see it was Graeme. They could settle things now; there was no need to wait.

He reached for her and cupped one cheek, kissing her the way she loved, a touch of his tongue, his warm lips, and a groan from him when he tugged her closer. He made her feel so special. He ended the kiss and whispered, "Did I wear you out last eve? You look tired, my sweet. Why do ye not take a nap?" He grasped her hands in his.

"Graeme, may I ask you some questions?" She had to hear his plans from his lips.

"Anything. Ye know I'd do anything for ye." He wrapped his hands around her waist and lifted her up, setting her on the bed before sitting down beside her. "What has you so anxious this morn?"

She took a deep breath and plowed forward. "Issy. I need to know about Issy. I fear she may not be well. My drawing skills arenae the best. Mayhap ye'll not be able to find Issy." Since he'd said he would do anything for her, she decided to push further. "Would ye take me there today? I could lead ye to the hidden entrance in the curtain wall, and we could sneak into the cellars and find Issy. Her father never visits her. We could come and go without being seen."

He took her hand in his, rubbing his thumb across the soft skin on the back of her hand. "There's no need to worry about Issy. We'll find her, Catherine. Two days is not so long to wait. On the morrow, I'd like to sit with you and my brother in my solar and have ye tell us all ye know about the keep. Ye may know something more important than ye think."

"It has already been several days." She squeezed her eyes tight, but the tears managed to stream through her lids. "She's so sick. Two days could be too late. Please, could we not leave today? I need to see her."

His hand came up to her cheek, and he brushed the back of his fingers across it in the lightest of caresses. She tipped her head toward his hand, wanting so much more from this man, but she could already tell he'd made up his mind. This wasn't to be, at least not until everything was over.

Graeme feathered kisses down her cheek before he spoke. "I've made the decision to leave ye here. I cannae worry about ye while I'm searching for Issy or your husband."

"But I'm the only one who knows exactly what she looks like and where she's kept. What if ye cannae find her? What if they have moved her? I would know whom to speak with about her whereabouts. You would have no idea."

"Catherine, war is no place for a beautiful lady."

"But I'll dress as a lad again," she said, speaking faster now, desperate to convince him. "I'll help ye find my husband. He tells his men they must fight ahead of him. He willnae risk his own death, so he hides in the keep. I can be of assistance to you… And then I could find Margaret and free her."

"I'll find him the same way I would if I'd not met you. We had planned to attack him a few days after I found ye in the woods. But we were forced to change our plans when we learned his men were out searching for you."

She reached for his hands, grabbing both wrists. "Please, Graeme. I am so worried about Issy. I have loved our time together, but my mind is overtaken with fear."

He stood from the bed. "I'm sorry, but I cannae worry about ye getting caught and possibly killed in the skirmish. Ye are safer here. Ye must trust me in this. I'll find your daughter and bring her to you." His tone was final, and his eyes were colder than they usually were when he looked at her. He'd made up his mind. "I cannot make any other promises to ye other than your daughter. I have no plans to kill the women and children, but I know not what will happen with his family. Margaret is his blood, Wesley is his heir."

"But ye promised to save Issy and she is of Henry's blood. Please, I beg ye not to do this. Please spare Margaret and Wesley. They are nothing like Henry."

"My sweet, I cannae promise to save them. My warriors will want their death as justice for my mother and brother. I will consider your request, but I make no promises other than your daughter. There are many unknown factors to an attack, and I will not make promises unless I am sure I can keep them."

She stood and turned her back to him, moving over to stare out the window to give herself the chance to think. He was forcing her to leave on her own. She had no choice—she would do what she had to do to save her child.

Graeme would be furious. She hoped he would forgive her in time, but she had to treat this as if he would not. She pivoted back to face him.

"I accept it, Graeme. May I ask something else of you?"

Graeme nodded, though she did not miss the quick look of surprise that passed over his features. "Make love to me. Please? I miss ye already." She would cherish this last time together.

He stepped closer and took her in his arms. "I cannae get enough of ye either, lass."

He kissed her and she threw her arms around his neck and melded her body to his.

Her favorite place to be—one last time.

CHAPTER TEN

CATHERINE LEANED ON HER ELBOW in bed, watching him as he dressed. He raised an eyebrow at her, the corners of his mouth curling.

"Ye like to watch me dress, my sweet?"

"Aye, I do. Your body is quite pleasing to my eyes. Ye have wonderful muscles in your arms, even in your legs."

"If ye dinnae stop looking at me as if ye'll be having me for dinner, I'll not be able to leave."

As she watched, his erection grew underneath the plaid he'd just put in place, pushing at the heavy fabric. She snickered, pleased with this new power she possessed.

"Laugh at me, and that will quickly rid me of my hardness."

She laughed harder and kneeled on the bed, falling toward him until he caught her in his arms, just as she'd known he would. "I shall let ye go, but not before I tell ye something. I love you, Graeme MacGregor. Ye are the nicest thing that has ever happened to me."

Graeme cupped her face in his hands and stared at her, his eyes transfixing her. He did not have to say it back, but she knew he felt the same. He had spent so long fighting every hint of softness in himself that he could not put his own feelings into words. The look in his eyes told her all she need know. He kissed her, a kiss so soft that she sighed.

"Ye please me more than anyone ever has, sweet Catherine. But I must go. We have much to plan." He gave her another quick kiss, then hurried out the door, still putting his sword in place. Before he closed the door behind him, he glanced over his shoulder at her and waggled his eyebrows, grinning suggestively. Oh, she would treasure the memory of these last moments.

As soon as he was gone, she knew what she had to do. She'd pack a few items to take with her, change into the lad's clothing she'd kept, and leave through the tunnel Rory had shown her. There was no other way. Unsure of where the tunnel would take her, she hoped she'd find a horse somewhere along the way. The horse she'd started out with had to be out there.

When she was ready, she pushed the rug aside and opened the trap door. She dropped into the darkness below and then reached up for the lit candleholder she'd set on the floor where she could reach it.

How she prayed it would stay lit.

She crept down the stairs, able to find her footing at the base of the steps because of the light emanating from the open trap door. Moving slowly to ensure her candle was not snuffed out by a breeze, she followed the passageway in the only direction it led.

The path took a turn not far from the beginning, but then stayed straight for a while. The farther she walked, the more cobwebs she encountered and the damper the darkness felt. She stayed to the middle of the path, trying to huddle into an even smaller figure, squealing when something scurrying along the ground brushed against her boot. Her heartbeat was moving so quickly that anyone standing close to her would likely be able to hear the pounding in her chest. She took two deep breaths before continuing along her path.

Three times she'd almost decided to go back, but she forged ahead, the memory of Issy's bright smile motivating her. She walked straight into a cluster of cobwebs and screamed, her hand flailing around her head, hoping the spiders did not land on her skin. Though she shifted the candle in front of her in the hopes it would burn some of the cobwebs, it was so slow going that it was not practical. She kept walking. Isbeil needed her. Each time she walked into her daughter's room, the wee lass held up her arms, a sign that she wished to be picked up and cuddled.

Who had cuddled her daughter while she was away? The poor child had no idea where her mother had gone or when she would return, *if* she would return, and her husband and his mother had no doubt told her lies. She had to stop several times to calm her racing heart, but each time she did, she said the same thing to prompt herself to move again.

"*Mama's coming, Issy.*"

Her heart broke at having to leave Graeme in such a fashion, but despite what she'd said to him, he did not understand her need to get back to her daughter. In truth, she was ashamed by the length of time she'd already been away from Isbeil, primarily because of a wonderful man who'd shown her a part of life she hadn't known existed. She reminded herself that she'd also had to be certain that her husband's guards were not still searching for her, but that did not change her guilt.

She could forget her daughter no longer.

When she finally made it to the end of the path, she attempted to open the door, but it was stuck. It probably had not been opened in months, perhaps years. She put her shoulder to the door and pushed, but it did not move.

After getting this far through the mice and cobwebs, her frustration and fears got the best of her and she burst into tears, suddenly so angry that she punched the door over and over again as hard as she could. Her candle flickered out from all her movement, so she tossed it to the ground, having no way to light it.

After four more pushes, the door finally started to give way. When she was able, she shoved it open and stepped out into the forest, hoping no one was around.

But her hope was shattered not a moment later. There on horseback sat a lone rider, staring directly at her.

Graeme MacGregor. He did not look pleased.

Graeme had rushed down the staircase after their sweet lovemaking, only to stop and think. It had just hit him. Catherine had told him that she loved him. Something in his chest swelled, a sensation he did not altogether understand. He ran into the kitchens to grab something to eat before he headed out to join his warriors.

Love. Did he love her? Honestly, he was unsure—it was still so new—but he had not responded to her declaration the way he should have. He decided to go back one last time to kiss her senseless, just because he wished to, before he saw to his men. He could already imagine the looks Tomag and Conn would give him for arriving so late in the lists. Once he gobbled down the bread he'd found, he stepped back into the great hall, pausing to think before deciding to give in to his whim.

He dashed up the stairs, taking three steps at a time, and flung the door open.

He froze.

In the corner of the room, the rug was pulled back, and the trap door to the escape tunnel was open. What the hell? He scanned the room, hoping to find Catherine asleep or hidden in the corner, but he didn't. Of course he didn't.

Catherine had run away. How had she known about the tunnel? Pushing that thought to the back of his mind, he focused on what he needed to do at that moment.

Should he go in after her? He'd been gone several minutes at least, who knew how far down the tunnel she'd be.

His decision made, he hurried out the door and flew down the staircase, fury consuming him as he ran. The only way he was certain to catch her was if he waited at the end of the tunnel. He knew that hidden passage well. Dark, dank, full of critters and spiders, she would be moving slow at best. In fact, he'd be surprised if she made it all the way through without turning back screaming.

He made it to the lists and shouted, "Conn, gather four men and meet me at the end of the meadow. Be ready to ride. Tomag, you're in charge until we return."

He was able to mount his horse in a flash because his stable lad had seen him coming. He had about four minutes to consider his choices, though he thought he'd already decided.

He'd asked Conn and the others to meet him at the end of the meadow because he meant to take her back to her husband. Now, no delay.

Aye, he could consider sneaking in the back entrance of the Merrill's castle with her as she'd requested. By going through the tunnel, though, she'd told him she did not trust him. He'd promised to rescue her daughter in two days. What was two more days? She'd already been here longer than that.

Of course, he'd told her she could not travel with them when they attacked the Merrill. While he knew her choice had been motivated by a wish to see her daughter, it still meant that she did not trust him. She could not love him if she did not trust him. Her professed love was a lie.

His mind tried to unravel dozens of different thoughts, ideas, and fears as he rode to the place where the tunnel came out to the west of his keep. He sat on his horse waiting…and waiting…and his stomach fell to his toes, sick over all that had happened. He should have stayed away from the flame-haired siren. She'd turned all his thoughts upside-down, almost making him forget what he owed his clan, his parents, and himself.

Now furious, he had no doubt what he would do to the lying temptress. He'd demand that her husband meet him at the gates to the Merrill keep, and he'd deliver her to his hands.

A knocking sound echoed through the clearing, and he recognized that it came from the door, probably her fist banging on the old wood.

The door flew open and she almost fell to the ground. She stood, brushed her clothes off and scanned the area until she saw him. He moved his horse closer to her, close enough to see the fear in her eyes. Damn, but he hated that she feared him. He had not said anything yet, but… she had the right of the situation.

"Going somewhere, Catherine?" He remained on his horse in case he had to chase her.

"Graeme." She stared at the ground, and the tears started as if on cue. "I'm sorry. Forgive me, but I must see Issy. Ye dinnae understand the love of a mother for her child."

"Mayhap I do not, but I understand that ye clearly dinnae trust me. How can ye pledge love to someone ye do not trust?"

"I tried to talk ye into taking me today. I asked ye, Graeme. I'll beg ye now. Please help me find my daughter."

"Nay. Ye've demonstrated your true colors. I'll take ye back, but I'll return ye to the hands of your husband. We'll not go in through the back entrance." He held his hand out to her, wondering if she would come willingly or if she would fight him. To his surprise, her shoulders slumped and she trudged toward him, her head down, saying nothing.

This was not the fiery woman he had come to know. "Nae fight in ye, my lady?"

She shook her head when she reached his side, staring off into the distance.

"Ye arenae going to run off so I can chase ye with my horse?" He smirked.

Her voice came out in the barest of whispers. "Nay."

"Why not?"

When she lifted her gaze to meet his, he saw the pride had been restored to her eyes. "Because I know ye would never hurt me. I'll take the blame for the error of my ways. I fell in love with an honorable man, and I willnae apologize. I should not have stayed. I left Merrill land and put my life at risk for my daughter's life, and for what gain? I allowed ye to distract my purpose. 'Tis no one's fault but my own."

Damn, he wished she'd cursed him or tried to run, anything but this. Some of the fire he'd felt while galloping to the tunnel's exit had already left his veins.

She held her arm up to him and said, her breath hitching, "Take me back. I must see my daughter. I'll not run, just take me back. I must see her with my own eyes."

He pointed to a log and she did not hesitate to climb up on it so he could reach her better. He leaned over and grabbed her by the waist, setting her in front of him before he turned his horse around. She said nothing, just sat the horse with her back as straight as a regal queen, intentionally not touching him.

As soon as they reached the meadow, Graeme slowed his horse to speak to Conn. "We ride to Merrill land. I'll return her to the Merrill only."

"Ye have no plans to go inside yourself?"

"Nay. She goes back, and we leave. The rest of our plans do not change."

Conn glanced at Catherine, her gaze still focused straight ahead, ignoring both of them. "Ye trust she'll not tell her husband?"

"Aye. Besides, she does not know for sure when we will attack. Since she knows our original plan, we'll change it. I'll decide when we return, after I have another look at his castle."

Conn did not offer any other comments, just nodded, so Graeme tugged on the reins and flicked them, leading the way into the forest. His brother stayed behind him, and their other guards fanned out around them.

They'd traveled in silence, Catherine's back as straight as the side of his curtain wall. Her begging had not commenced when they left MacGregor land, so he guessed it never would. He tried to come up with something to say to her, some way to let her know that while she'd hurt his feelings, he admired her tenacity for sticking to her original goal, but the words never came.

They lived in two different worlds. True, they'd crossed over for a couple of days, but it could not last forever.

Later that afternoon, they arrived at the front gates of the Merrill castle. "We need to see the Merrill," Graeme barked out.

"For what purpose?"

"I've found his wife, but I will return her only to his hands."

"Ye will wait and we'll advise him."

The closer they'd come to Merrill land, the more rest-less Catherine had become. When they reached the gates, she squirmed in front of him and refused to look at her husband's guards. He was silently glad she didn't look at them. They had strange expressions, as if it gave them some twisted pleasure to see her. It reminded him of the look of the men he'd killed—their sick excitement about Merrill's promise that they could sample her. For a quick moment, he wished to tug her close and turn his horse around, but he did not.

It was too late.

Several minutes later, the gates opened and Henry Mer-rill came out on horseback. The expression on his face caused Catherine to start shaking, and for the first time since he'd come upon her outside the tunnel, she leaned back against him. He could feel the trembling course through her body as her husband silently ran his gaze from the top of his head to her toes.

After a long pause, the Merrill said, "Catherine. Are you hale?"

She nodded, but did not lift her gaze to her husband.

"Where did you find my wife?"

"She was in the forest being chased by a boar."

Her husband smiled. "Should have allowed the boar to have her."

Graeme could not help but feel the bristles rise up on his back. "Ye have nae respect for your wife, Merrill?"

"MacGregor, I'll thank you for returning her, then I'll tell you to get off my land."

Graeme nodded and lifted Catherine off his horse, though he had to admit, it was much harder than he'd expected. As angry and hurt as he still felt, he did not wish to give her up—especially not to *him*.

He never took his eyes off Henry Merrill. Memories of

that day returned to him violently, reminding him of his purpose.

But the moment he lowered Catherine to the ground, the Merrill jumped down from his horse and struck her so hard she fell to the ground. "Ye worthless whore. Did ye use your whoring ways on him? Ye probably carry his seed."

Catherine stayed down, the smartest thing to do, and the Merrill did not move to strike her again. Graeme turned his horse around, ignoring the raging feeling in his middle, and nodded to his warriors. They had started to gallop away when a voice carried back to him.

He turned his horse around in time to see Catherine stand and square her shoulders before speaking to her husband. The fire in her eyes had returned. His brave spit-fire spoke, "I left to try to find a healer for our daughter who ye care nothing about."

Her husband struck her again, but Catherine did not even cry out. Instead, she ground out, "I left for our daughter, but this man saved me. If ye wish to know the truth, I did lie with him, and now…"

Merrill struck her again. Graeme spurred his horse—intent on killing the bastard—but Conn's voice brought him back to reality. "Graeme, remember your promise."

It would be the death of them all if he tried such a thing.

Catherine finished, "…I know what I've been missing. I have no regrets." She wiped the blood from the corner of her mouth from her husband's last strike. All was quiet.

Graeme stopped his horse next to Catherine and whispered to Merrill, "Strike her again and I'll see ye tortured for your cowardly ways."

Merrill climbed on his horse and said to his second, "Innes, bring her inside."

Graeme fought everything inside him that told him to

slay the man in front of him. He glanced at Conn, who gave him a short signal to hold his fury. He knew why. The bastard was goading them in the hopes they would strike out, giving him a reason to have his men kill them in cold blood.

If Graeme called the devils down on them, Rory and Boyd would be left alone. His clan would not get the resolution they needed and deserved.

Though every fiber of his being told him to steal her away again, he turned his horse around and left. As soon as they were far enough away not to be overheard, Conn yelled at him, "Ye saved us from a bloodbath. I thought your cock would overtake your sense. We were outnumbered and ye knew it. Six to over a hundred. There was naught we could do."

Graeme turned to his brother. "I'll kill the bastard. Tomorrow we attack."

Conn smiled. "Wise choice. Now ye are making sense. 'Tis time to finish this."

CHAPTER ELEVEN

C ATHERINE STAYED ON THE GROUND after her
husband struck her. She heard the sound of horses
retreating. Graeme and his men headed home.

Graeme clearly hated her now. For some odd reason,
she could not fault or resent him. Until she'd given birth
to Issy, she'd had no idea how much it was possible to love
a child. Her love for her daughter drove her more than
anything else she'd ever seen or done.

The happiness she'd enjoyed with Graeme was a gift
she'd only been allowed to keep for a short time, but she
would treasure it. She wished she could be angry at him
for returning her to her husband, but he was a man who
thrived on loyalty, and she'd chosen to leave him.

She thought of what she'd said to Henry. Until today,
she had never once spoken back to him, and now she'd
insulted him in front of his men. He would make her pay
for that affront, there was no doubt of that, but she hoped
to find herself carrying. Inside of her was the seed of a
good man. She would pray every night that Graeme's seed
had taken.

After they arrived in the bailey, her husband gripped
her by the hair and yanked backward. "Get moving, you

wench. Ye whored your way into my enemy's bed? You'll see what you get for that."

He pushed her toward his second, Innes. "Ten lashes at the main post for the whore. Do it at dusk this eve. Take her to the dungeon."

She said nothing to her husband and followed Innes inside the keep. He chuckled all the way down the staircase, then stopped at the bottom when everyone else was out of earshot. He spun around and twisted her breast brutally. "I'll have a fine time whipping ye, lass. I cannae wait to see if ye are carrying. If ye are ripe with the MacGregor's seed, I'll have ye whenever I want. Your husband willnae care about ye at all if that happens."

He moved toward the end of the passageway, pulling her along. She would keep her mouth closed until she discovered how her dear Issy fared. He threw her in the cell her husband had built last year, hoping to fill it with prisoners. She moved inside, not looking over her shoulder until she heard the clang of the door closing and the sound of the key in the lock.

Innes winked at her. "Until later, wench."

The cell was small, but not as small as she'd thought. Four or five prisoners would easily fit inside. There was a bucket of water near the door, and another empty bucket by the far wall, presumably for relieving herself. Several manacles adorned two walls, some up high and some low to the floor, and she shivered involuntarily at the thought of being chained to the wall down here. There was one stool, so she sat down, her hand moving up to see how badly her cheek was swelling from her husband's strikes. She winced at the small pressure, then dropped her hand. It would heal like the others.

How she hoped someone would come and tell her about her sweet daughter. She did not have to wait long before Dolag stuck her face against the slats. "My lady? 'Tis true? Ye are hale and hearty?"

She rushed to the metal door. "Dolag. Issy? How is she?"

"Och, my lady. She is the same. No better, but she misses ye terribly. I'll tell her ye'll see her soon. No matter how angry my lord becomes, he'll allow ye to see her. I hear ye will be getting a lashing? Please say 'tis not true. Ye are too sweet."

"Aye, 'tis true, and I go willingly. He usually allows me to see her after a punishment. I will gladly take ten lashes to hold my lass again." Tears erupted and she allowed them to run freely down her cheeks. "Tell her how much her mama loves her, please?"

A sound echoed from down the corridor. Dolag jumped and turned her head.

Catherine maneuvered her hand between the slats and pushed her away. "Go, Dolag, go. I dinnae wish to have ye hurt for me."

Dolag disappeared and Catherine fell to the floor, curling into a ball and sobbing her heart out. When her tears were spent, she closed her eyes and fell asleep.

When she awakened, it took a moment for her to recall the events of the afternoon. Her husband's bellowing broke through her cloudy mind.

"Up, you whore. It's time for your punishment." The door opened and Henry grabbed her by the hair, yanking her to her feet. "Take her, Innes. And make every lash count."

Catherine was so eager for her daughter, she could not stop herself from asking, "My lord, Issy? Could I please stop…"

His hand swung out and caught her in the side of her head, slamming it against the stone wall. She saw stars for a moment, but fought to stay conscious.

"No, you will not see Isbeil. You have embarrassed me beyond anyone's imagination. I am forced to discipline you so that I can keep order in my castle." His brown hair needed cutting, but Henry Merrill was still a fine-looking man, though not as fine as Graeme MacGregor.

Innes tied her wrists together and dragged her up the stairway and out into the courtyard. She glanced around only once, wishing to see how many had come out to watch her moment of humiliation.

Too many. She closed her eyes, refusing to look. Innes led her to the post and pulled her arms over her head, hooking the rope that held her wrists together on a nail above her head, positioning her so her back faced out.

"Ten lashes is your punishment for leaving. Commence now." Henry's voice echoed over the chanting of the crowd. She heard male and female voices alike; the crowd was daft, bloodthirsty, and many of them started cheering after the first lash. Catherine quelled the need to scream, but could not stop her knees from crumpling underneath her at the sheer pain rippling through her body. Though she fought for control, after the second lash, she screamed and screamed and screamed. Another two lashes sliced into her skin before she leaned her head against the wooden post and whimpered, "Graeme, help me."

Fortunately, no one heard her through the crowd.

Graeme had discussed all with his men, and they planned to attack the Merrills the following day, a few hours before dusk, hoping to catch them unsuspecting and maybe deep in their cups.

He'd hidden his guilt from his brothers, though his men had all expressed their opinions about the way the Merrill had cruelly struck Catherine, openly discussing what they would like to do to a man who could treat a woman so.

But Graeme hid everything. He couldn't tell them how close he was to vomiting over leaving his Catherine with the bastard.

How he chastised himself every minute.

How he wished he would have stopped the Merrill's cruelty.

How much he missed her.

Or how much it pained him to think of her in the hands of such a twisted man.

He'd get her out. He'd save her and the girl.

At the end of his planning session with the men, Graeme made his way back to the keep. Rory followed him silently, but when Graeme fell into a chair in front of his hearth, the lad stood in front of him.

"Graeme?"

"What is it, Rory?"

"There's something I need to tell ye."

Graeme held his head in his hands, not interested in listening to what his brother had to say about Catherine. He knew the lad did not approve. Hellfire, he didn't approve of what he'd done either. "What is it?" He lifted his gaze to his brother, surprised to see the devastated look on his face. "Rory?"

"My fault. 'Tis all my fault."

"What?"

"The tunnel. I showed her. I thought if the Merrill came for her, she would need a place to hide, so I told her about it. 'Tis all my fault she left, and all my fault ye took her back to that bastard. My fault her husband struck her." Rory's moist eyes told Graeme just how burdened the lad felt.

"Rory, she would have gone back for Issy anyway. And trust me, it wasnae the first time the man has struck her."

"Aye, but she snuck out. If she hadn't snuck out, ye would not be so angry with her. And ye would not be back to the way ye were before Catherine. And I liked ye better when she was here. Boyd did, too. I wish to go with ye when ye bring her back. Please?"

Graeme brought his hands up to cover his eyes. What could he say to his brother to ease his conscience?

"She would have found another way. Ye did not open the door for her or push her into the dark. She did that herself. 'Tis no' your fault."

"Why would she go back if he's beaten her before? I dinnae understand. Ye were kind to her."

Graeme stared at his youngest brother, still innocent in many ways. He rubbed his chin as he did his best to reason through Catherine's mind. "She was drawn back to the keep by her daughter. She's a wee, sick lassie of four summers, and Catherine could not bear to be away from her any longer. I guess she was willing to accept his beatings so long as she could be with her daughter."

"I dinnae understand that." He appeared to be calming down, fortunately.

"Neither do I, Rory."

"Forgive me, Graeme?"

"Aye, I forgive ye, lad. Go to bed. 'Twill be a busy day on the morrow."

Rory nodded and turned to leave.

"Rory?" He stood up, his hands on his hips.

"Aye?"

"I liked me better when she was around, too."

Rory grinned. "She's nice. I like the two of ye together. She likes ye, too. I could tell the way she watched ye."

"Go to bed."

Rory turned and raced up the staircase.

He was alone finally. He moved over to the hearth and

leaned his hands on the stone mantel above it, staring into the flames. All he could think of was his flame-haired beauty—and how he'd lost her.

Conn came into the hall, followed by a stranger. "Graeme, there's something ye need to hear."

Graeme turned around, resting his leg on a stool and leaning his elbow on his knee. He was tired. What was this about?

The man nodded, fumbling with his plaid—a Merrill plaid, Graeme just now noticed.

Graeme settled his foot back on the floor, his heart beating faster in his chest. "Aye? Ye have news or a message?"

"News. Catherine, the woman ye returned, the Merrill's wife? He had her savagely lashed in front of all today. When she collapsed, the brute kicked her. I couldnae… my sire taught me to respect women, ne'er to raise a hand to them because we were so much bigger and stronger. It sickens me to see what he does to his wife. I respectfully request to join your clan. I have no respect for this plaid."

"Can ye tell us the layout of the Merrill castle?"

"Aye. Most of it. I've not been in the laird's chambers or the dungeon, but I know about where they are. 'Tis where she is being kept now."

"The dungeon? They put a woman in the dungeon?" Conn asked, glancing at Graeme.

"Aye, manacled her like an animal."

"Your name?" Graeme did his best to hide his fury, not wanting to frighten this man away. He could be quite helpful to them.

"Heck."

"Heck, welcome to the clan. I willnae allow ye to know our secrets until ye prove yourself, but I'd be pleased to have ye draw a map of the keep if ye could."

"Aye. I'll do it. I'll do it now. Anything if ye'll take me

in."

"Find him the tools he needs, Conn."

When his brother headed off to the solar, Graeme turned back to Heck. "Where is the back entrance to the curtain wall?" Catherine had told him where it was, but he thought he'd test the man.

"In the southeast corner, my laird."

"I have one other request for you. I'd like to set one of my own men inside the Merrill's castle. I need informa-tion. Do ye think you could do that for me? Could ye talk someone into allowing a new warrior in?" Graeme wanted to send someone inside to watch over Catherine, tell him exactly how she fared. He had to know if the Merrill threatened her life.

"Aye, I'll do it, my laird. He's lost many guards, so he's eager to take on new ones. I know exactly who to talk with to get him inside."

"Once ye finish with the map, Conn will take ye to the warrior." He reviewed his instructions with Heck and finished just as Conn returned and set the necessary tools down on the trestle table.

Graeme updated Conn on his plan then moved toward the door. He needed to get out and think. "Conn, I'll be back in a few minutes. I need to take a walk."

Conn nodded. "I'll take care of this. I thought ye might need a ride after what ye heard. Head down to the loch and back. Clear your head. You'll need it on the morrow."

Graeme left the keep and headed to the stables, deciding to take his brother's suggestion. He saddled Starlight and cantered out to the loch. Once there, he dismounted and sat down beside the water, watching it. Much to his sur-prise, he felt his eyes grow heavy, so he settled back against the rock behind him for a quick nap.

Green eyes and red hair danced through his mind just

before he fell asleep.

He had no idea how long he'd slept, but a soft voice called to him. "Graeme, help me." He bolted off the ground, spinning around to see who had called to him. No one was there. Feeling daft, he raced around the loch, expecting to see someone there, yet he knew in his heart he would not find anyone.

It had been Catherine calling to him.

His Catherine. He rubbed the sleep from his eyes and thought hard. He wanted her out of there before they attacked. The others would think him mad, but his mind was made up. He'd sneak her out overnight, bring her here to tend her wounds before Merrill and his men ever found out. And if he could get her daughter out with her, he'd do it.

There was no point in waking anyone up to tell them where he was headed. They'd insist on coming with him, and this was something he needed to do alone. He mounted his horse and left.

Two hours later, he was on Merrill land, but still a fair distance to the keep. He decided to take a different route, hoping to avoid discovery. Once he drew near, he dismounted and left his horse in an area where the animal could graze while he was gone. He rubbed his neck and patted his flank. "You'll wait for me, will ye not?"

He meandered his way through the trees until he found the curtain wall. The door was in the southeast corner, just as he'd been told, and he crept inside, allowing his eyes to adjust to the dark. He'd only gone a short distance before his head was struck from behind. He fell to the ground swinging, but darkness overtook him.

The next time he awakened, Merrill's second stood in front of him, both fists clenched as he laughed. "Och, ye are awake. Good. I prefer to have a man watch me beat him to death. Hold him, lads."

That was when Graeme realized three men were holding him while Innes punched him. Two others stood behind Innes, and one of them was Merrill. He did not have a chance.

What a fool he'd been.

CHAPTER TWELVE

CATHERINE LIFTED HER HEAD WHEN she heard the key in the lock. Someone rushed over to her side. She heard Benneit's voice. "Here, my lady. Your husband is allowing you a pallet and two blankets. Forgive me for the restraint tying your foot to the wall, but Innes insisted."

Margaret came in behind Benneit. "Dear Catherine, what has my brother done to you? Had I known, I would have stopped it myself."

Catherine was in too much pain to smile. She tried to sit up, but one leg would not move.

Margaret fussed around her, attempting to make her more comfortable. "My brother has lost control," she said, her voice shaking. "He's the one who belongs in the dungeon. Catherine…"

Even in the dim light, Catherine caught the pity in Margaret's eyes as her gaze finally settled on Catherine's back. "He's daft…mad and daft. Here, allow me to help you get comfortable and then I shall place the ointment on her wounds. Benneit, I know you are trying to assist her, but we must respect her sense of decency."

Benneit nodded. "My lady, do not pull," he said to Catherine. "If ye pull against the rope, your tender skin will become raw just as your wrists are. Please do not hurt yourself any more. There is no reason for you to be closer to the door."

Benneit lifted her up enough for Margaret to slide the pallet underneath her, careful not to touch her wounds. He helped her move to a comfortable position on her belly, if there was such a thing. At least the pallet was an improvement over the cold stone floor. She rested her head on the pillow and sighed, wishing she would fall asleep and wake up a sennight from now back in Graeme's bed. Margaret finished applying the salve while Benneit fussed over the rest of her accommodations, grumbling and snorting as he did his best to clean the area.

After Margaret was done, Benneit whispered, "My lady, I'll cover you with a blanket, but if 'tis too painful, tell me. It may hurt at first from your wounds, but mayhap it will not be too painful once it's in place."

The moment the blanket descended across her shoulders, she had to grit her teeth against the pain. "Please, no blanket," she groaned. "Just place it over my legs, Benneit. And please move the water closer. I cannae move that far."

"Of course, my lady."

"Issy? You'll care for Issy?"

Margaret clasped her hands in hers. "Of course, Catherine. I love Issy as if she were my own. I would never allow Henry to hurt her. Do not worry about her."

"My thanks, Margaret." She left the small cell, but not before Catherine saw the tears in her eyes. Margaret was as true a sister to her as her dear sister Anna was when she'd been at home. How she missed Anna. Her heart was so torn, not knowing what to do. Should she tell them what Graeme planned? If Margaret told her brother, everything could change, and he'd be on the offensive, possibly killing more MacGregors. She could not risk sending Henry

Merrill on another killing rampage. If he was capable of it seven years ago, he was capable of the same today.

Nay, she had to believe that Graeme would do the right thing once the moment came. She believed he was a good man, an honorable Highlander with Scots blood. He would not kill women and children. She had to believe in him with a conviction that would not waver.

She had to if she loved him with all her heart.

Benneit grabbed the bucket and lifted the ladle, filled to the brim with fresh water from the well, and held it to her lips. "Drink. Ye must drink, or you'll never make it out of here. I'll not leave until ye drink." She sighed and did as he asked, though she was not interested in the least.

She took one sip, swallowed, and tried to push him away.

"One more for Isbeil? Please?"

She peered up at her loyal manservant, then nodded, swallowing as much water as she could. "Leave it nearby."

He did as she asked and left.

A short time later, a commotion came from the end of the passageway. She closed her eyes, hoping she would be ignored. The sounds of several footsteps carried toward her along with a few voices, the first one her husband's.

"Keep him alive so I can fight him in the courtyard. All I need is for him to stand, then I'll slay him in front of witnesses who will swear he attacked me first. Do not wait until he has much strength back." Then she heard him chuckle. "He landed a few good punches on ye, Innes."

Innes retorted, "Aye, but I paid him back—and then some."

"He's a fighter," another said.

She kept her eyes closed until she heard the key in the lock. They were putting another prisoner in with her? Saints above, how could they put a man in here with her?

She knew the answer. When it was built, they probably

hadn't planned on needing a separate cell for a woman. Before she had more than a moment to think on it, they were inside the cell. They dumped the man's body near the wall and shackled his hands and feet, all four of them. It was unlikely he'd be able to touch her. She noticed a familiar shock of brown hair before she snapped her eyes shut.

It could not be him.

Her eyes had deceived her for sure. She was eager to look again, but refused to do so until the guards left.

The sound of the metal door shutting and locking was followed by the shuffle of retreating footsteps, and Catherine finally opened her eyes again. There was only one torch in the passageway, so it was hard for her to make out his features, but she had to know for sure. The man never moved, probably unconscious from his beating.

She crawled over on her belly as far as she could with her foot still tethered to the wall. When she was close enough, she gasped. "Graeme?" A little closer and she sighed, recognizing the man she had given her heart to, though his face was full of cuts and bruises, his lips swollen and bleeding. He lay flat on his back, hands tethered to one wall and feet to another. She wiggled and squirmed until she was able to rest her head over his shoulder, letting out another sigh when she breathed in his beloved scent. "Oh, Graeme. What have ye done?"

With her tether and his bindings, this was the only way they could touch—her head to his shoulder. She attempted several other positions, but this was as close as she could get.

She rested her head on his shoulder again. "Graeme?" Tears filled her eyes because she knew he wouldn't answer. She stared up at the wall, wondering how their lives could have brought them to this terrible point. Tears rolled down her cheek and she tilted her head back to stare at him. How she loved him. For some odd reason, she was comforted by his presence despite what his imprisonment meant for both of them. She reached with one arm and brushed his hair back from his face. He stirred and pulled back when she hit a large swelling in the back of his head. She placed her lips on his, careful not to hurt him where his lip was split, and whispered, "Forgive me."

His lips responded to hers, kissing her gently. She opened her eyes to find him staring at her. "Nay. Forgive me. I should not have sent ye to the wolf. Ye are hurting?"

"Aye," she whispered. "He had me whipped, but now I'll stay here until he determines if I'm carrying your bairn. 'Tis a better place than his bed. Did ye come alone?"

"Aye. I heard ye call my name in my sleep. I had to come." His voice grew a bit louder.

She placed her finger on his lips. "Shhhh. I do not want them to hear ye. Do Tomag and Conn know ye are here?" She hoped his answer would be aye. If so, they would come for him soon. There was hope.

"Nay. I told no one. I thought I could get past his guards by coming in the back way."

"Still. They will come for ye, aye? We have hope?"

"Aye, but it could be a day or two before they determine where I am."

She scuttled back over to find the ladle and give him water. Most of it fell over the side of his mouth. "Lift your head, Graeme. I'll hold it to your mouth, and ye should drink all you can. We know not what will happen on the morrow."

Graeme swallowed what he could, then set his head back down on the cold stone. "Your daughter?"

"I have not seen her yet, but my manservant says her condition is unchanged. That pleases me."

"Good. Catherine?"

She put the ladle back, then looked to see what he wanted.

"Place your head back on my shoulder. I want to breathe in your scent. Know ye are near."

She did as he asked. "Do ye think we'll make it out?"

"We'll make it out. The only thing that could prevent it is if we die from the fever."

"Nay. We must survive."

"If we die together, worse things could happen."

She snuggled closer to him and closed her eyes. "I love ye, Graeme."

If her eyes had been open, she would have seen him smile.

❧

Graeme opened his eyes in confusion. Where was he? What had happened? He was unable to move his arms or his legs, and he hurt everywhere.

He was cold, so cold. He was never cold. What had changed?

A woman's voice called to him. "Graeme? Ye have the fever. Drink this. Please?"

He shook his head.

"Please, Graeme? Ye could die if ye do not eat or drink. Please do it for me."

He gave her a puzzled look—he wasn't sure who she was, but he knew she was special. When she came close, he smiled. "Catherine, my wee Catherine. I love ye, Catherine."

❧

Catherine dropped the ladle at his declaration. This wasn't exactly how she had wished to first hear those words from him, but she'd accept them any way she could. She kissed his forehead. "I love you, too, Graeme Mac-Gregor, and I will forever."

"We shall have forever together, Catherine. Did ye not know that?"

She was so choked up that she could not speak. It tore her apart to see her strong warrior humbled. "Aye. Forever."

His eyes looked glazed and sick. She tried two more times to get him to drink, but he refused. "Graeme, please drink, *please*!"

Before he spoke, he would close his eyes and then open them again. Whenever his gaze would fall on her, he burst into a smile. Mayhap he did love her.

"Catherine? Did ye know we are soulmates? 'Tis what we are called."

"Soulmates? I've not heard that expression before. Who told ye this?"

His eyes fluttered shut again. "Who told ye, Graeme?"

He did not open his eyes this time, but smiled at her nonetheless. "The angel. She said we are soulmates. That we belong together. I tried to go home, but she said ye needed me."

"Home?" Poor Graeme was delirious from the fever. She'd heard of people talking daft when the fever took over. She'd never seen it set in so fast, but what else could cause him to talk of such foolishness?

"Aye. I wished to go to heaven, but she turned me away. Promised I would not regret coming back to ye."

She placed a chaste kiss on his forehead. A gasp escaped her when she felt his burning skin beneath her lips.

His eyes fluttered open again. "Did I tell ye that I saw my sire, too? He told me 'twas too early. I have much to do for my brothers and my clan yet. He said to listen to

Tomag."

Catherine had no idea what to make of his strange dec-larations. She mopped his brow with a cloth dipped in water, wishing there was more she could do for him.

"I'm glad I came back for ye." He closed his eyes and fell fast asleep.

Benneit cleared his throat outside the door. He'd come to check on her a while back, bringing fresh water, not long after her husband's men had thrown Graeme into the cell. "My lady, he has awakened?"

"Aye, but he makes no sense. He talks of angels and going home."

"Trust me, 'tis not a good sign if he feels he's been called home. Did ye get any water inside him?"

"Nay, he refuses me." She settled her hand on the side of his head, running her fingers through his matted hair.

"My lady, ye must make him drink. Men with the fever will die without water."

She lifted her head to stare at her manservant. "Truly?"

"Aye. I've seen it happen many times. If ye can get them to drink, they have a chance. I must go. Force it upon him, or he'll die."

"Benneit, I must ask a favor."

"Anything, my lady."

"I do not wish to risk your good standing, but 'twould it be possible for ye to steal the key?"

"My lady, ye are in no shape to leave. Ye'll not get very far, wounded as you are." He shook his head. "And ye know what your husband would say if I set you free."

"Not for me. When Graeme awakens, I wish to set *him* free."

"Why? 'Twill only bring trouble on your shoulders. Ye know how your husband is."

"Because he saved my life after I left the castle to find

a healer for Issy, and then he came back for me. My husband has hurt him and his family enough. Ye know he killed Graeme's parents and brother?"

Benneit stared at the floor. "Aye, I've heard whispers."

"I'll not stand by and allow Henry to kill Graeme. 'Tis wrong what he suffers, and I wish to set it right." She could not find a good way to explain to her manservant why she was so compelled to help him. No one else could understand how driven she was to save this man—her conscience and her intuition and her heart all calling for her to do the same thing.

A sound came from the end of the passageway. Benneit's eyes widened and he whispered, "I'll see what I can do, but only for you, my lady." He spun on his heel and left without another word.

She listened to Benneit's retreating footsteps. What more could she do?

She continued to watch over Graeme, but his eyes danced beneath their lids as he slept. Sometimes he frowned; other times he smiled. When his eyes stopped moving, she whispered, "I love ye, Graeme MacGregor. Come back to me, please?" She feared he was letting go. The fever raged inside him, and his breathing had become so shallow it frightened her. Was it because he slept deeply or because he was taking his last breaths? She could not stop thinking about the warning from Benneit. If she didn't get him to drink, he could die…and then she would not need any key.

That thought terrified her, spurring her into action. She grabbed his shoulder and shook him with all her might, ignoring the pain in her own back. "Graeme, wake up."

He frowned, but he did not open his eyes.

She tried again. "Graeme!"

He still did not change.

"Please, Graeme. Wake up for me. I wish for one kiss from ye. Please?" Tears rolled down her cheeks at the thought of losing him, watching him take his last breath in front of her. "If you're my soulmate, ye cannae leave me, not yet!"

To her surprise, he tipped his lips toward her. She leaned in to kiss him, not risking a delay.

He kissed her back!

Hope blossomed through her belly. "Kiss me, Graeme."

He smirked and kissed her again, this time teasing her with his tongue. She ended the kiss and stared at him.

Suddenly, she had an idea.

CHAPTER THIRTEEN

CATHERINE FILLED THE LADLE AND held it close to her mouth. Graeme still had not opened his eyes, but appeared to be sleeping again.

She held the full ladle near her mouth and whispered to him. "Kiss me again, Graeme."

He tipped his lips toward her as he'd done before. She filled her mouth with the water and put her lips to his, waiting for him to tease her with his tongue. *Come, Graeme.*

As soon as his tongue touched her lips, she moved her head so it was over his and opened her lips, allowing the water to fall into his mouth. She was careful to give him just a bit until she heard him swallow, but then she gave him more. She moved her hand up to his throat so she could feel him swallow, even massaging it lightly to encourage him.

He took all the water in her mouth. She wished to shout to the heavens, but she waited to make sure he kept it down.

She continued to do the same every quarter hour, giving him the chance to take it on his own, and if not, she would feed it to him. Unfortunately, after several rounds, she fell asleep.

Graeme swam in the loch, but it was the warmest water he'd ever known. He rolled onto his back, kicked his feet, and stared up at the blue sky, feeling the heat of the sun warm his body. A soft voice called to him, and he rolled onto his belly, searching for its owner. There she was, the woman he loved with all his heart.

Catherine. She stood in the sand at the side of the loch, though he'd never seen a loch with white sand. She beckoned to him, so he swam toward her until his feet touched the bottom of the loch.

His brother's voice called to him, too, but he did not see him. "Rory?"

"Graeme, where are ye? We cannae find ye." He could see the tears in his wee brother's eyes.

"Here, Rory. I'm with Catherine. Can ye not see us?" He hollered to Rory, but the vision of his brother faded out, quickly replaced by Catherine at the edge of the loch.

He stood up, his shoulders popping above the water level—the water a brilliant shade of blue unlike any loch he'd seen in Scotland. Catherine stood on the sand in front of lush trees unknown to him. She wore no top, her breasts full and bountiful, but a long, flowery skirt was tied at her hip. Her red hair fell in long waves down her back. What a beauty she was.

His life had changed for the better the day Catherine walked into it. He couldn't help but recall how he'd taken his men to see the Merrill based on his intuition and the Highland breeze. That intuition had told him the day would be special, but he hadn't realized the truth. Some stronger power had guided him to Catherine, *not* Merrill. They were meant to meet, to be together, to finally join their souls. He stepped toward her, but he didn't seem to move forward. He could see her hand motioning for him to come forward, but his feet did not seem to work.

He stared at her, confused. "I'm trying, Catherine. I cannae reach you."

She whispered, "Then I'll come to you." As she came closer, he saw that she carried a brown bowl made from tree bark, filled with clear liquid. He wanted to touch her, to be with her, but he was losing strength, and by the time she reached his side, he slipped and fell against her.

"I cannae make it."

"Aye, ye can. Ye must drink this. Trust me the way I trust ye." She held the bowl to his lips and he drank. "If ye drink this, then I'll give ye a kiss."

He smiled, remembering how sweet she tasted. She set the bowl to his lips again and he drank heartily before coughing and waggling his brow at her.

She smiled. "Aye, ye've won a kiss." She set her lips on his and he drank her sweet nectar, wanting more and more.

He belonged with Catherine.

Forever.

When she awakened, he was staring at her. She picked her head up to see if she'd imagined it. "Graeme?"

"Is it you, Catherine?"

"Aye, 'tis me." Why did she suddenly feel as if they'd had this conversation before, perhaps a thousand times?

"My love, ye are as lovely in the dark of a dungeon as ye are in the light of the hot sun."

Catherine stared at this man as if she'd never seen him before…and yet…it also felt as if she'd seen him more times than she could remember. Which was it? The warmth in his eyes wrapped around her, pulling her away from the cold dungeon, from her hard life, beckoning her to trust him and join him in something better. She envisioned them running through a Highland meadow in summer, Isbeil following along with them, able to keep up. In her vision, Catherine laughed as he picked her up and swung her in a circle, Issy clapping her hands and jumping up and down as she hadn't done since she was a wee bairn.

Staring into his blue eyes transported her to a place of the same color, silver stars sparkling in the background, yet there was nothing beneath them in this place, nor could she tell where he stopped and she started. Clouds passed by them and through them, leaving her with a sense of contentment she'd never known.

And just like that, the vision disappeared, but she was compelled to touch him. She placed her hand on his forehead. "Your fever is gone?"

"I had the fever? I do not recall. In fact, I dinnae know how I got here. The last I recall is coming inside the bastard's curtain wall."

She rested her head on his shoulder and kissed his chin, closing her eyes, reciting a quick prayer to God for saving him.

"How long have I been here?" He tugged on his bindings, but they did not give.

"I honestly dinnae know. I was put here when ye… when I returned. They brought ye in late that night. I have not counted the number of nights since then."

"Why do ye wince so, my sweet? Are ye still hurting?"

There was no reason to lie to him. He could not do anything more than she could. They were stuck here together. "My back is sore from the lashing."

"Catherine, my sweet Catherine. Forgive me. 'Tis my fault for returning ye here." His fingers reached for her, but he was unable to touch her.

"Do ye feel strong, Graeme?"

"Strong? Nay. But with a sword, I could get us away. Why do ye ask?"

"When last Benneit was here, I asked him to steal the key to the lock. Mayhap we can set ye free." Her voice dropped to a mere whisper, lest she be overheard.

"I'll not leave without ye."

"But I am unable to move, and I'll not leave without Issy. Ye could get help, come back later."

He thought for a long pause. His gaze held hers, and a deep sadness struck her to her core. She did not wish to be parted from him either. "Please, Graeme. 'Tis our only chance."

He moved his legs, then his arms. "I'll be stiff, but I believe I'll be able to get free. Can he give me a weapon? A dirk or dagger?"

"I'll speak to Benneit when he comes. Until then, ye must eat. Ye have not eaten in days. 'Twill help build your strength."

He wiggled his hands and pursed his lips, shrugging his shoulders.

"Aye, I'll feed you. I have saved some bread." She maneuvered back to her pallet and pulled out the small loaf she had hidden under her blanket. When she returned to him, his eyes were full of fury.

"What's wrong?" She held a piece of bread out to him, and he took it.

When he finished, he said, "I saw your back. Tell Benneit to free me. I'll kill the bastard with my bare hands."

Catherine thought he might be too furious to listen to her, but now that he was of sound mind again, it was her opportunity to beg him to reconsider his plans. "We must talk first."

"We may not have much time. Speak quickly. I wish to leave as soon as possible. I know not how long I've been gone or where my brothers are."

She placed her fingers on his lips and whispered, "Hush. Ye do not wish to anger anyone, or I shall pay the price."

He stopped instantly, his gaze softening at her declaration. "Say what ye wish."

"Benneit can only come on the sly, so we must wait patiently for him to arrive, though I know 'tis difficult. Until that time, I wish to plead with you."

"Why plead? Ye know I'd do anything for you."

"I understand your need for your clan to see justice served. Watching your parents' death must haunt you every day. I cannae blame ye, but please leave all the innocents alone. There are guards who are good men, servants who have known no other home. Your clan has lost many people. Why not offer a place for Henry's people? When they see how ye treat them, they will serve ye well."

She paused and took a deep breath. "And I would beg ye not to kill his sister, Margaret, and her son. She is a widow, and Wesley is a lad of six summers. They're nothing like him. Allow them to find another home, if your people will no' accept them."

"I will confess to ye. My clan wants Merrill's family dead, but I struggle with what is right. Please dinnae ask me to save the men here, because I willnae. I wish to slay the ones at the gate who looked at ye wrong. Your husband has fed them lies for years. We will kill any warriors who try to stop us, just as the Merrill did when he attacked my clan. I'll agree to sparing the servants. My men will be able to accept this since they've done no wrong. They will be happy to welcome women into our clan, but Henry's family? I'm sparing ye and Isbeil, I cannae promise to spare his mother, his sister, and her son.

This seems a fair exchange for saving you, and fair for the death of my mother and brother."

He pressed a hand to his forehead as if his thoughts pained him. "If Tomag had not been out hunting with a group of warriors, we would have been lost. When they returned, I thought Tomag would go mad he was so over-wrought with grief. Those warriors are the ones who buried my family, who have shared my grief. They survived, but they bear a great amount of guilt for not being there to help us. Tomag believes they could have stopped your husband."

"Ye do not?"

"Nay." He closed his eyes. "I recall how many men the Merrill had, many more than he has now. He did not kill all in the village, I know not how he chose. But vengeance is necessary for my clan to heal."

"Benneit says many have left because of my husband's cruelty. He has worsened each year, but that does not matter. What matters to me is this. There are many fine people who live here. You've said you'll spare the rest of the women and children, Graeme. Margaret and Wesley don't deserve to die."

"I will consider your words about Margaret and her bairn," Graeme whispered. "But I'm sorry. When we attack, we will kill the warriors and anyone else who tries to stop us."

"Ye must exercise some restraint, Graeme, or ye are no better than my husband."

Their gazes locked and they stared at each other for quite some time. She could tell that he did not believe all she said. She did her best to hide the tears that erupted from her eyes at the thought of so many deaths. It hurt to think of all that pain and loss, and of Graeme bearing the burden of it. His clan needed revenge, but to what end?

"Please, Graeme. Reconsider. Ye need not do this. Duel with my husband alone. He's the one who wronged you. Leave the others, please."

"For you, I'll reconsider. But I make no promises. And ye know many of his warriors must die, or we will never get to him. Can ye not understand that?"

Tears blurred her eyes, and she could not answer. She'd done what she could to convince him. Perhaps on his own, he would be able to see what is right. She'd leave him to his own thoughts. Graeme MacGregor was a good man. She had to believe in him, trust him to do what was right.

They stared at each other for a few more moments. His voice carried over to her, low and husky with emotion. "Why do ye love me, Catherine? I plan to do what ye hate."

She rested her head on his shoulder again. "How can I no' love you? Ye have given me things I've never known." She ran her finger down his arm, tethered above his head. "Ye touch me with a tenderness that is so strange to me, especially when it comes from the same hand that can kill so easily. Ye have whispered sweet words in my ear, and held me with the gentleness shown to a newly born bairn. Ye make me scream your name with pleasure."

She wished he would look at her, but his gaze was averted.

"But look what I did to ye? Ye should hate me for bringing ye back to the beast."

"I was a fool. I should have trusted ye. Instead, we are now in this predicament."

"I thank ye for forgiving me, and I vow to get ye away from the brute." He brought his gaze back to hers. "I promise you."

"Ah, Graeme, who is to know what would have been

the best path for us? They say everything works out in ways ye least expect. Mayhap destiny brought us here for a reason. But whatever happens, I know that I am grateful for our short time together." She placed a soft kiss against his neck and fell asleep, listening to the lilt of his breathing.

Several hours later, Benneit crept down the passageway. When he arrived, she heard the key in the lock and turned her head. Night had fallen, so she hoped her husband's warriors were deep in their cups.

Bennett whispered, "I have the key, my lady. Are ye sure ye wish for me to set him free?"

"Aye." She pivoted to glance at Graeme, pleased to see him awake and ready to be freed.

"Many thanks to ye, Benneit," Graeme said as the manservant worked on his manacles and bindings.

"I do this for my lady, not for ye. Listen carefully. I have given the men along the way an extra potion in their ale. Most of them sleep, but 'tis a delicate thing to choose the correct amount of powder. I know not how long 'twill last. Ye must hurry out the back opening in the curtain wall. I will lead ye that far."

While Benneit worked his bindings and Graeme stretched his muscles, tense after being bound for so long, he whispered to her, "Come with me, Catherine. I will protect ye."

She shook her head. "Nay, I stay with my daughter. If ye are successful, we will be waiting for you."

"I have something for you." He reached inside his tunic and pulled out a necklace. "This belonged to my mother. I would like ye to have it. She would have loved ye had she had the chance to meet you."

Catherine fingered the silver chain in her hand, a round pendant at the end, swirls of silver dancing around a small blue stone in the center. "Graeme, 'tis beautiful. This should belong to your wife someday."

"I never hoped to find someone as loving and giving as you. My mother would be proud of my choice. If we both make it to safety and you are free, I will be on my knees begging you to marry me. Please keep it as my troth to you."

Catherine's eyes misted as she ran her fingers across the cool metal. Then, looking into Graeme's eyes, she slipped it over her neck. "I wear it to honor your mother and her life, that she raised ye and brought ye into my life so I could understand true love."

Graeme kissed her forehead, rubbed his limbs, and finally stepped away from her, ready to follow Benneit.

"Graeme. One boon for your freedom?"

He spun around. "Ask for anything other than changing my life's purpose, and 'tis yours."

She wished to taste him one last time. True, they'd kissed when he was delirious, but he hadn't been himself. "One kiss."

She watched his eyes soften as he strode back to her. She was able to stand because she was still tethered by only one leg. He cupped her face and said, "Gladly. Nothing would please me more."

His lips descended on hers and he kissed her, a kiss unlike any they'd shared before. It was a kiss of need, of desperation and longing, and of love—she was sure of it. He ended the kiss and she whispered, "Go. Godspeed to ye on your journey."

"I will return for you and Issy. Do ye trust me?"

She closed her eyes and immediately felt the feather-light touch of his lips on each lid. "Ye must trust me, lass. I promise to think on all you've said."

Could she? Could she trust a man who could kill innocent people, even if he thought he had just cause?

Aye, she could—she trusted that he would do exactly as he promised. "I trust you. Now go and do not tarry."

He placed a chaste kiss on her lips and headed out of the cell, never looking back.

She crumpled to her pallet and cried herself to sleep.

Graeme followed Benneit down the passageway, though he moved at such a slow pace, he was stunned. How long had he been bound to that wall? He'd thought maybe a couple of days, but the stiffness of his muscles told him it might be more.

Whenever they neared a guard, Benneit would hold his hand up to stop him, then the servant would check that the guard was unconscious before they continued to move forward. They traveled past many guards, all slumped over, moving through an intricate maze that he'd never have been able to maneuver alone. There were too many turns, too many paths.

He owed Benneit, and he owed Catherine.

When they reached the end, Benneit slipped a small blade into his hand and pointed to the door. Before Graeme left him, he clasped the man's shoulder and nodded to him, a signal of his appreciation and recognition for what he'd done.

"Not for you," Benneit repeated again. "For her. Ye owe her your life, too."

He frowned, unsure what that meant, but Benneit explained without waiting for his response. "When ye had the fever, she fed ye water from her own lips. Ye'd be dead by now if she had not. I've seen many others die from the same condition without water. She saved ye. Do not forget that. Get her away from here—her and the wee lass."

Graeme nodded, but then hustled out the back entrance. Recalling he was at the southeast corner of the castle, he headed in the direction from which he'd come. He ran and ran as fast as he could, praying he would get away before being discovered.

But his stamina waned so quickly, he knew not what to do. He stopped for water at a small burn, refreshed himself, and followed the burn, hoping to find his horse. His mind began to blur and his steps slowed. Where the hell was his horse? He'd left him not far from here, had he not? Spinning in a circle, he searched everywhere, through the forest and the nearby valley, but there was no sign of Starlight. His horse had left him.

How long had he been gone? He pushed ahead, praying he could find his way to the edge of MacGregor land. If he could make it that far, eventually one of his own guards would come upon him.

An hour later, his mind clouding, he slowed his journey to search for something to eat. When had he last eaten? Wiping the sweat from his brow, he searched for anything at all, ready to shout to the heavens when he found a small apple tree. The apples, unfortunately, were too high in the tree for him to reach, and though he tried to climb it, he didn't have the strength. When he caught his breath, he'd search the grass for an apple or two. He had just let himself collapse to the ground, his back sliding against the tree, when he heard the sound of horses not far away.

Dammit, but he'd have to hide. He could barely push himself to his feet, but he managed to find a clump of bushes to hide in. He'd just managed to fall to the ground when he heard his brother's voice.

All he could do was crawl out of the bushes, trying to wave his hand at his brother and his warriors as they crashed through the trees, galloping right past him. Seven of them, if he counted correctly. Unfortunately, they did not see him. He put his fingers to his lips and let out the loudest whistle he could. The last two horses slowed, but only one turned around.

Tomag.

Tomag let out a yell to stop the rest of their men. Graeme's loyal second dismounted and raced to his side, and Graeme could swear he noticed tears in his eyes. "Saints above, but ye are a sight for these poor eyes that have been searching for ye for hours, lad."

He was helping him to his feet when the other men arrived with their horses. Conn said, "Graeme? Who the hell did that to ye?"

He slumped against his second, and the last thing he heard was Conn's voice. "Get him on your horse, Tomag. We need to get him home."

CHAPTER FOURTEEN

GRAEME OPENED HIS EYES, SURPRISED to dis-cover he was in his own chamber. Every part of him ached, but he was glad to see he was home and not in that foul dungeon. But then he recalled who he'd left behind. *Catherine.* He rolled onto his side, swearing, struggling to get up so he could rally his men to go with him to bring Catherine and her daughter to safety. Unfortunately, his limbs would not listen.

Rory sat on a stool by his side. "Graeme? Ye are hale? I'll get Conn."

He ran out the door before Graeme could stop him to ask for a drink, his lips so dry that he could peel the skin from them if he tried. Pushing himself up in his bed, he let out a sharp yell when the pain of his injuries hit him.

Conn and Tomag shoved into his chamber. "Ye'll live, ye wily bastard?" Tomag asked with a smile.

"Aye, I'll live. Water?" He pointed to the urn on the chest. "Did Starlight find his way back?"

"Aye, 'tis how we knew ye were in trouble," Tomag said.

Conn handed the water to him and sat on the stool next to the bed. Rory stuck his head back in the door, his hair all askew from his run, and Conn gave him more instructions before the lad could speak. "Rory, get him some porridge, bread, or broth. Whatever is there."

"He'll live?" Rory squeaked out.

"Of course, I'll live. Do ye think ye'd get rid of me, Rory? I'm hungry as a wild boar. Find me something good, will ye not?"

As soon as Rory left, Conn said, "Tell us all before he returns."

Graeme settled a pillow behind himself and leaned back. "Not much to tell. I went to kill the Merrill for beating Catherine, and I was hit over the head, beaten, manacled, and bound in his dungeon. Her manservant drugged several of the guards and set me free. How long have I been gone?"

"Three days. Did ye see Catherine?"

Graeme took another swig of water and said, "Aye. She was tethered next to me in the dungeon."

"'Tis true he put his wife in the dungeon? Twisted bastard." Tomag paced at the end of the bed.

"Had her whipped first."

"Your thoughts?" Conn asked. "Did ye learn enough to help us?"

"We go for the Merrill, but we will kill any who try to stop us. I know where to find Catherine and her daughter."

"What about his family?" Conn asked. "What are your plans for them?"

"Catherine said his sister has helped her. I know not what I should do—what the clan wants. I feel I should kill her as he did our mother, but Catherine begs me to save her and her son. He has an elderly mother there, but Catherine does not beg for her life."

Conn asked, "She must be nasty like her son. Kill the mother and the sister, spare the lad."

Tomag crossed his arms. "I understand your confusion, but I wish to say something that ye both need to think on."

"What? I welcome your guidance." He'd promised Catherine to reconsider, to think on her words, and he would.

Tomag looked at the two brothers. "I know we've all begged for justice and to kill all. This has given us the need to see this finished, but now that it is nigh, I wish to bring up an alternative. I want ye to ask yourselves what your sire would do, and remember your honor as a Highlander. Ye must be always able to live with your decisions, to be able to tell another Scot why ye did what ye did. If ye dinnae, 'twill haunt ye for the rest of your life. Do not worry about your warriors. Ye have their respect, and they'll follow your lead."

"But what if they disagree with us?" Conn asked.

"Think on what the warriors thought of your sire. Would they have argued with him if they disagreed with him?"

Graeme looked at his brother to see his reaction. Conn looked as startled as he felt. Both of them knew the answer to the question of course—their sire's men had never questioned him—but Graeme had never thought of it that way. The warriors' approval had seemed so important to him because this wasn't just about his personal desire for revenge on Merrill; he was seeking retribution for their whole clan.

Tomag said, "Aye, I see I have given ye something to think on. Ye are the laird now, and the men look to ye the same way. Consider that while ye heal."

Graeme scowled. "Heal? We attack on the morrow."

"Hold on to that thought, fool." Tomag held his hand out in front of him.

"On what thought?"

Rory came in and gave Graeme a hunk of bread and some cheese, along with a bowl of mutton stew.

"On the thought that ye are ready to fight. Ye need a day or two to rest and get your strength back. I doubt ye plan to stay back, do ye?"

Graeme snorted.

"Just as I suspected." Tomag crossed his arms. "I'll beat ye myself if ye try to go back by the morrow. Ye need to heal."

Rory stared at Graeme, a strange expression on his face.

"What is it, Rory?" Conn asked.

"Graeme, ye look bad. Ye are all bruised and blue and purple. Your lip is cut and your face and…"

"Rory. I'll be fine."

"Papa was watching over ye," Rory whispered.

Graeme was about to put a bite of stew in his mouth when he froze. "What did ye say?" A quick vision of his sire filled his mind.

Rory repeated, "Papa was watching over ye, or Mama, or Alpin. Ye look near to death, ye do. How did ye escape? Ye had to be helped. Look at your wrists where ye were bound. You're all bloody. Are your ankles the same?"

Why did he have a sudden recollection of talking with his sire? Had he dreamed of his father? The memory danced at the edges of his mind. Hadn't his father told him he had much to do?

Graeme pulled his legs out from beneath the covers to check. "I guess so. I'll be fine, lad. Dinnae worry."

Then he remembered. His head jerked up to stare at Tomag.

"What is it, lad?" Tomag asked. "Is something wrong?"

"Nay," he whispered. He could not tell him about his dream, about his sire advising him to listen to Tomag.

They'd all think him daft. Well, all except for Boyd—he thought Boyd might understand if he were here.

Conn said, "Rory, get a tub bath up here for him."

"A tub bath? Have ye lost your mind, Conn?" Graeme bellowed.

Tomag leaned over the bed, placing his hands on the covers on either side of Graeme's legs. "Nay, he's no' lost his mind. Ye have. And here's how 'twill be. Ye will eat that food while Rory gets the tub and water. And if ye dinnae soak in that tub, your whole body will be infected with the pus. You're filthy and ye smell, and ye will die for sure if ye dinnae listen to us. Now, we'll be happy to discuss our strategy on the morrow, but we'll not be attacking until the day after or later, depending on your strength. For now, ye'll eat and wash yourself, and then Moyra will change those sheets, bandage ye where necessary, and ye'll sleep again. Once ye've done that, we'll talk—not before."

The door opened and Moyra stepped inside, gasping when her gaze settled on Graeme. "Oh my, Graeme."

"Ye have the right of it, Moyra. What would ye suggest for his wounds?" Conn asked, glancing past Tomag.

"Two tub baths. One to get the filth and the crusted blood off, and another with clean water to wash."

Tomag said, "Then that's what we'll do. See to it, Moyra. If ye need help holding the lad in the tub, call me and I'll sit on him."

"Like hell," Graeme shouted. "I'll not take two baths like a bairn, and we're attacking tomorrow. I'm going back for Catherine."

"And how do ye aim to do that?" Conn asked, his arms crossed in front of him.

Graeme pushed himself out of the bed, trying to push his way around his brother. The only problem was, he couldn't. He tried a second time before falling back onto the bed, cursing.

"Raise your arms," Moyra said, making her way across the room to him. He stood so he could help Moyra peel his tunic off him. Pain radiated through him since the fabric was stuck in all his wounds.

She threw his plaid and tunic outside the door, and all he could do was let himself fall back onto the bed again. Two lads brought the tub in, and two others filled it with water. Once they left, Rory came back inside.

Graeme tried to stand and immediately collapsed. "Dammit."

"Ye haven't enough strength to push me around, my laird," Moyra said, clucking her tongue. "I think ye should listen to Conn and Tomag."

He sighed, agreeing with her. He couldn't move. "Since ye seem to have the right of it, Tomag, send a small group to the land of Catherine's sire, Clyde of Beaton. He sold her to the Merrill. She has not been home since then. Go and assess. She had one sister she was fond of, and she wonders about her mother. I'd also be interested in word of the healer Catherine sought for her daughter. Just gather information, 'tis all I want."

He moved to the edge of his bed and whispered, "I'm all yours, Moyra. I'd be pleased if ye'd do what ye could to help me heal quickly."

Graeme allowed his brothers to help him into the tub, leaned back, and promptly fell asleep.

Catherine sat up and stared at the opening in the door, waiting to see who was approaching. Her back still hurt terribly, despite all the poultices Benneit had applied to it, but the clicks she heard had a distinct sound.

The sound of her husband's boots. He had a way of

sashaying and hitting the stone with the heels of his boots such that his footsteps rang out with a most distinctive sound. She'd learned to recognize and fear that sound. The key fumbled in the lock, and then he stepped inside, a twisted expression on his face, made worse by his smile. "So, my dear. Your manservant betrayed me. You convinced him to drug my warriors and set your lover free, hm? Were you not happy coupling with him here in the dirt every day?"

"What?" Catherine couldn't think of another thing to say. What had he done with Benneit?

"You shall not see Benneit again. I've taken care of him."

Her eyes filled with tears. Her beloved Benneit. What else would happen to him, to her, to all the people she cared about?

"Allow me to introduce ye to your new manservant. This is Jabari. Ye'll not be getting away with anything with him. He cannae hear or speak, so cry for help as much as you'd like—you'll never be able to sway him. I'll leave him with you."

The sound of his boots echoed as he exited the chamber. She stared at the door to her cell, waiting to see her new manservant.

The largest man she'd ever seen appeared in the doorway. She gasped because he'd startled her so. But it wasn't the size that frightened her. After all, Graeme and his next eldest brother were both huge men.

This man was different. He had to duck to step inside her cell, and he filled the doorway. His arms were like tree trunks and he had a gold ring in one ear, but that was not what had surprised her. This man was unlike anyone she'd ever seen before.

She stood up and took a step forward. His head was shaved and his skin was brown.

He stood still, staring at her the same way she stared at him. He grinned at her.

He did not look so frightful with that smile on his face. She decided to try what she could.

"Jabari, would ye please help me visit with my daughter?"

His smile turned to a scowl. He immediately stepped back into the passageway, locking the door to her cell behind him.

Catherine closed her eyes and dropped herself back onto the dirty pallet, worrying once again about her dear Benneit. Where was he?

CHAPTER FIFTEEN

THE NEXT TIME GRAEME AWAKENED, the sun was just moving above the horizon. He'd slept most of the day away. He rolled onto his side, noticing he was alone in his chamber.

He did not like that one bit. His hand fell to the spot where Catherine had slept, his heart swelling with the wish that he could bring her back with just a thought and a prayer. A spot in his chest ached, and he rubbed it without thinking.

No amount of rubbing would make this ache leave him. He ached for Catherine. She had become a part of him, and they belonged together—if he had his choice, they'd always be as closely wound as they'd been in that dungeon. Though they had been chained to opposite sides of the small cell, once they'd discovered Catherine could stretch out just far enough to rest her head on his shoulder, they'd spent the rest of their time together touching. Close enough for him to breathe in her scent, to feel the silky strands of her hair against his cheek, to listen to the sound of her rhythmic breathing while she slept.

He tried not to think of all she'd gone through, the whipping, the beating, the cruelty of her husband—all because of him. He'd brought her back to a deranged laird, one who should not be allowed to live, and Graeme only wished he could kill the man twice: once for his family and clan and once for the woman he would make his wife.

But this time, he would do things carefully. He would strategize and listen to his warriors, his brother, and his second. In honor of the woman he would make his wife, he might even give in to her tender sensibilities and spare more of Merrill's people than he'd planned. Mayhap even his mother and sister. Something told him she was correct. Catherine spoke of righteousness, of fair treatment. Tomag had spoken of the honor of Highlanders, of the Scots, of pride, and he reminded him of something he oft forgot.

He was laird of the MacGregor clan, and he would do what was right.

A soft knock sounded at his door. He attempted to get out of bed, but his legs would still not follow his commands. He ran his hand through his hair, frustrated with his own weakness, and said, "Enter."

The door opened slowly, and a face peeked around the corner.

Boyd?

"Boyd, please come in. Close the door, if ye like." Though stunned that his brother had walked out of his chamber and found him, he did not wish to frighten him away.

Boyd stepped in, hesitant at first, but then closed the door. He sat on the stool next to the bed, and brought his gaze up to Graeme's. In a voice crackly from disuse, Boyd whispered, "Ye will live?"

"Aye," Graeme nodded, trying to show that he was hale. "I will heal. Dinnae worry about me. Henry Merrill cannae take me down for long."

Boyd processed this information and Graeme noticed the corners of his mouth curve upward, almost to a smile. But then he stopped and frowned. "Catherine?"

"Catherine?" Graeme pushed himself up in bed so he was almost sitting with his back against the wall. "Catherine is not here yet, but I will go for her and bring her back."

Boyd thought for a moment, and then moved to the other side of the bed and sat down, choosing the very spot where Catherine had slept. "I will wait for her."

"Ye liked her, Boyd? I do, too."

Boyd said, "Love her."

Graeme sighed and nodded his head slowly. "I love her, too. Dinnae worry. We'll bring her back."

Boyd curled on his side until he was comfortable. Another knock sounded and his other two brothers came in, not waiting for him to bid them enter.

Conn was clearly agitated. "Graeme, Boyd is not in his chamber." Once inside the chamber, he glanced at the other side of the bed and froze. "Boyd?"

Graeme nodded. "Boyd just joined me. He's decided to stay in here until Catherine returns."

Rory rushed to Boyd's side and clasped his shoulder. "When she returns, Catherine will marry Graeme."

Graeme gave Rory the greatest glare he could muster. He did plan on marrying Catherine; he simply didn't want to do or say anything that might send Boyd away. This was a major change in his behavior. He'd left his room, alone, and found another.

Rory said, "Ye should marry her, Graeme."

"Mayhap I will, but do not send Boyd away."

Boyd grabbed his hand and said, "Aye, marry Catherine."

Conn looked at him and grinned. "Boyd always was the smart one."

Boyd laughed.

The following morning, Graeme pulled himself out of bed, pleased to see much of his strength had returned. He'd finally made it down to the great hall the eve before, and he'd eaten two bowls of stew while both Rory and Boyd watched in fascination, laughing at his appetite. Graeme had waited until most of their warriors had finished their meal, not wishing to make an issue of his return—or Boyd's. His brother had followed him downstairs and stayed, even eating some bread with him. They were all more than pleased with the lad's progress.

When Graeme descended the stairs now, he saw that many of his warriors were breaking their fast. It was time to speak to them, to discuss his plans.

He stood at his dais and held his arms up for silence. "Many thanks for being by my side through these difficult times. I've decided that we shall attack Henry Merrill this eve. We'll wait until a couple of hours before dark. I wish to come against them when they least expect an attack, and I'm hoping a few of his warriors will have already overindulged in ale or be abed with a woman to distract them.

"Eat hearty, and be prepared to leave later today. I give ye final details later, after I discuss the details with Conn and Tomag in my solar. Merrill's life ends this eve at my hands, and I do so in honor of my sire, my mother, my brother Alpin, and for all the MacGregors."

The hall erupted in cheers and shouts, all his men jumping to their feet to applaud his decision. He smiled and made his way through the crowd. His brother and Tomag had already slipped away from the crowd, and they were waiting for him in the solar.

Tomag nodded to him as soon as he closed the door behind him. "'Tis good news and a good decision, my laird."

Once they were seated, he turned to Tomag, who had returned from his journey just before breakfast. "What did ye discover?"

"Her mother no longer lives," Tomag replied, "but her sister does, and is unmarried. Beautiful lass, though not as pretty as Catherine. And the healer she sought is no longer there."

Graeme's gaze narrowed. "Get on with it."

Tomag smirked, but his expression changed to a frown a moment later. "Her sire is a mean bastard."

"His name again?" Conn asked.

"Clyde Beaton. Nasty man. 'Tis true that I'm become soft in my old age. For much of the journey home, all I could think of was that Catherine's short life has been spent with two bastards. Beaton's two sons stood by him, fools much like their sire. All of them barking orders at the sister, though she appears unharmed. Not a happy lass. They say the mother died a year ago, just fell asleep in her bed and never woke up."

Graeme couldn't help but agree with Tomag's assessment. "It all fits. I've not changed my mind. We end this tonight, no matter how long it takes. I would prefer to take them unsuspecting by sneaking around their curtain wall in the dark. We'll scale their wall and attack from all directions. 'Tis the only way to do this."

A knock sounded at the door. "Enter," Conn said.

Rory came in, Boyd behind him. Though it surprised him that his two younger brothers wished to join the meeting, he was also quite pleased.

"We attack this eve?" Rory asked. "'Tis what the men are saying."

"We do. Rory, mayhap 'twould be best if ye stayed back with Boyd. I am in need of some men to protect our keep. What say ye?" Graeme hoped the lad would come to his own conclusion about why he'd made the request. Boyd would not wish to be left alone.

Rory glanced at Boyd, whose face lit up.

"We'll protect it," Boyd whispered. "You'll take me outside later, Rory?"

Conn and Graeme both waited expectantly, hoping Rory could see the importance of the duty that had just been thrust on his shoulders. They were finally going to bring their brother back into their world.

Rory lifted his chin and puffed his chest out. "Aye, 'twould be our honor to protect our keep, my laird. Boyd and I accept."

Graeme hid his relief, and Conn ambled over to clasp Boyd on the shoulder. "We trust ye two to do a fine job. We'll leave a score of warriors behind to take your instructions, Rory."

Both of the lads smiled.

Later that day, Tomag organized their warriors, giving the men their final instructions. "On this day, the Mac-Gregor clan seeks vengeance for the death of our laird, his wife, and his son. We will seek out Henry Merrill, and kill any who try to stop this mission. Go and may the Lord be with us on this journey." Graeme said a quick prayer and mounted his horse, moving to the front of the army, Conn by his side. When he was ready, he nodded to his brother and his second, spurring his horse forward and letting out the MacGregor war whoop. Warriors on either side lifted the MacGregor flag, their shouts heard by all on their land.

Revenge was near.

When the Merrill castle came into view, Graeme pointed in the directions he wanted each team of his men to go. Groups of ten to twelve men headed to a dozen different areas around the curtain wall, all with rope ladders to assist with their climb. Using his bird signals, Graeme sent his men off to their tasks, perfectly choreographed as he'd been planning for many moons. This night would be the MacGregors' night.

Conn asked, "Kill all or hold them?"

Graeme stared straight ahead, a flame-haired beauty fresh in his mind. "Kill any warriors who stand in our way. Do not kill the women or children. Take them, and any who do not fight us, as prisoners."

He rode up to the gates, waiting for his men to get on the inside and open them. His plan was to head straight for Henry Merrill, then on to the dungeon to save Catherine.

Victory would be theirs.

CHAPTER SIXTEEN

C ATHERINE GRABBED HER BELLY BEFORE she bent over the bucket, heaving over it for the third time. It could mean one of two things.

She knew it was possible that she carried Graeme Mac-Gregor's babe, but it was too soon to be certain. It was also possible that her illness was from her poor conditions in the dungeon. The dampness made her disinterested in food, so she'd eaten little. Her mother's healer had told her how important it was to eat daily, especially for a woman who might be with child. She just couldn't stomach her provisions.

A part of her was ecstatic, but another part of her feared for her bairn's life if she was carrying. She ate little, fed only scraps that her manservant brought her on occasion. The door opened to her cell and Jabari stepped inside, narrowing his gaze at her as she wiped her mouth. He shook his head and grabbed both buckets before leaving and returning with fresh water. He grabbed a ladle and held it out to her, pointing to the water, then gave her a handful of mint leaves after she finished drinking.

The mint, while wonderful after heaving, only served to remind her of Graeme. How she missed him. Every night she wondered whether or not he'd made it back to Mac-Gregor land. How would she even know if he'd survived?

She'd know if he came for her, but it had been a couple of days and they'd heard nothing. He'd made her promise to trust him, and she did, but…would he return for her as soon as possible? How capable was he of returning? He'd been in bad shape when he left and had no horse. He could have met all kinds of danger outside these walls. But her worse fear had not happened, he hadn't been caught and returned to her cell.

What if her Graeme was dead?

She fell on her pallet and closed her eyes, falling asleep dreaming about a sweet man with dark locks and blue eyes, eyes that followed her wherever she traveled.

Eyes that loved her.

She awakened in the dark to shouts and screams coming from the courtyard. Before she could process any of it, shouts came from the end of the hallway.

Henry bolted down the passageway, shouting for Jabari. He unlocked the door and threw it open. Grabbing her by the arm, he said, "See what you've done? Your lover has attacked my castle and is killing everyone in his path. Not just our warriors—women and children and elderly, too. Jabari, get Isbeil and bring her along. We are leaving the castle through the tunnel."

Catherine could not believe her ears. Graeme was here with his warriors? Her first thought was that she had to find some way to stay behind, except Henry had just told Jabari to grab Issy.

Finally, she would see her daughter.

She followed her husband down the passageway, and Jabari met them at the end with a crying Isbeil in his arms, holding her like a sack of flour.

"Issy, 'tis Mama. Do no' cry, wee one. Where is Dolag?

Jabari, bring Dolag along."

"No," Henry slapped Catherine across the face. "Mind your tongue. You do not give orders. Dolag stays behind. She can die at the MacGregor's sword along with all the others."

They passed Dolag, who had burst into tears as soon as Henry had said she could die, and Catherine grabbed her hand to give it a squeeze of encouragement. Even if Henry's family and the men were all at risk, she had to believe Graeme would keep his word about sparing the rest of the women and children. Her husband shoved past Jabari. "Give the child to her mother," he said. "You must protect us. Kill anyone who tries to stop us." Jabari handed Issy over to her and then pulled his sword out of its sheath.

Catherine barely noticed—she was too busy kissing her daughter's sweet cheeks and doing her best to quiet her as they continued to rush down the passageway. "Hush, child. You're with Mama now. I'll protect you."

Henry's mother rushed out into the hall, and Henry gestured to her impatiently. "Follow along or you will probably die, but do not expect me to slow for you."

The old woman glared at everyone, but she joined the rear of their little group.

Henry shoved women and children out of his way as he ran into another chamber in the cellar. Shouts and screams of death met her ears from above. Graeme was here, possibly killing everyone in his path. She'd tried to convince him to show mercy to those who did not stand against him, but it seemed he had not listened to her. Tears flooded her cheeks as she heard the thump of bodies dropping to the floor above, and smells reached them that made her wish to lose her insides again, though her stomach was mostly empty now.

She had no time to think, just move, Jabari's hand

pushing her along gently on occasion. She followed her husband down a dank staircase into a dark passageway, just now noticing that he carried a bag of something. After a brief inspection, she guessed it to be a bag of gold coins, part of the wealth he was said to have. They ran and ran through an endless labyrinth of pathways, finally ending their voyage nearly an hour later at another staircase. They climbed and she fell twice, but Jabari helped her back to her feet both times. Rodina was a distance behind them, huffing and puffing and cursing through the maze.

"Once we exit, it is on your shoulders to take us to a safe place, you beast," Henry bellowed.

Jabari ignored him and moved toward the top, tugging Catherine behind him.

She did as instructed, crushing her daughter to her chest and whispering sweet, calming words in her ear. All Catherine could do was hold her tight, praying that Graeme would save her. Praying that he had done the right thing.

As they came to the top of the staircase, slits of moonlight spilled into the passageway. They made their way to the edge of a forest. Merrill ran in three directions before finally speaking to Jabari. "We must leave. MacGregor is killing and setting fire to my castle." He pointed at the dark tendrils of smoke rising in the sky.

"Where will we go, my lord?" Catherine had no idea what his plans were. The little knowledge she had of the area was that Merrill land bordered MacGregor land and Beaton land.

He stared at Jabari. "Head to Beaton land. Her sire will hole us up until this mess has cleared."

Rodina, struggling with each breath, collapsed to the ground. "I'll never make it. Go on without me. I'll find my way someday." She waved her son on.

Henry mumbled, "Fine, old woman. We're leaving."

She coughed and hacked, but then shouted after them. "If you were any kind of son, you would have your great lumbering guard carry me to safety."

Catherine noticed a tic in her husband's jaw that she'd learned not to ignore.

They moved on, but Rodina continued to pester her son. "I hope the MacGregor kills all of you."

Suddenly Henry stopped them. He turned around and headed back to his mother. Catherine was sure he'd finally found a bit of compassion for the woman who had birthed him.

How wrong she was. As soon as she saw her husband grab his sword, she turned Issy's eyes away and covered her ears. A moment later, a scream carried back to them. Catherine guessed the beast had just killed his own mother. Who would be next?

Catherine wanted to scream and scream, something she knew would only provoke him. So she stayed silent. Her husband was truly daft. She could not wait to be rid of the man, but she also had no wish to see her father.

No matter what challenges came next, her priority, as always, was to protect Issy.

She'd kill Henry if he tried to touch their daughter.

Graeme fought his way through the courtyard, heaving his claymore left and right, but he could tell he was not at his best yet. Being badly beaten and then held as prisoner in a dungeon had taken its toll on him. He would not give in.

Whenever he had the chance, he glanced around the inside of the keep, searching for the Merrill, but he had not seen him yet. The bastard's numbers were dwindling. Graeme was proud to see that all the hours his men had spent in the lists were now paying off.

He was almost to the hall when someone jumped in front of him, brandishing a weapon. "Well, we meet again, MacGregor. I see I planted a few good punches on ye." Innes grinned at him before he came straight at him.

The memory of several men holding him down while Innes pummeled him fueled his attack. "Aye, ye did. Should ye not be embarrassed to admit ye had to have several warriors hold me down to get your punches in? Ye could not handle me alone, weak man?"

Innes laughed. "We shall see who the weakest is."

He brought his sword overhead and drove it as hard as he could toward Graeme's head, but Graeme ducked at the last minute, swinging his claymore in from the side. He caught the bastard's arm, and the man's eyes widened, apparently stunned that Graeme had drawn blood. He could see the fury in Innes's gaze as he swung blindly. Graeme easily blocked the swings, surprised to see how each lacked the power of the last. He took one powerful lunge toward his opponent, knocking his weapon out of his hand, and then thrust his sword deep into the lout's belly.

He stood in front of him and whispered, "Who is the weakest now?"

It had been a death blow, but Innes was still conscious. He gave him a weak, pained grimace. "I wish I'd planted my sword in your sire, but I watched it. Who was the weak one then? You could do nothing to stop it."

Graeme twisted his sword in the man's belly before pulling his sword out and pushing him to the ground. "That's for the MacGregors and for Catherine."

There was no one else around him at that moment, so he wiped the sweat off his brow and headed toward the great hall. He shoved the door open, hoping to find more men cowering inside, but there were none to be seen. He headed straight for the kitchens off the hall, hoping to find the staircase to the store rooms in the cellars of the castle. Then he could make his way to the dungeons, to Issy. The stairs were where he'd hoped they'd be, and he rushed down them, only to freeze at the bottom. Servants lined the passageway, huddled together, some holding dirks, others sobbing. The fear on their faces saddened him, but it was to be expected.

He held one hand up to quiet them. "Drop your weapons and I'll not hurt ye."

Instantly, several dirks clattered to the stone floor.

"Kick them to the opposite side." They complied quickly.

He strode down the side of the passageway, eyeing each person, checking for Merrill or Catherine. He found an empty chamber and directed them all inside, surprised they fit.

"If ye dinnae take arms against my men, we will consider taking each of ye into our clan. The Merrill and his warriors will be dead by the morrow. I'm looking for your laird. I have not seen him on the outside, and he is not among ye. Then I look for the woman who was held in the dungeon."

A woman with dark hair and kind eyes spoke first. "The Merrill took Catherine and Issy and headed toward the underground tunnels not long ago. His mother and his new guard followed."

"Your name?"

"Dolag, my lord."

Graeme recognized her as Catherine's maid. He would bring her back to his keep. A man stepped forward and said, "I can lead ye there, if ye like."

It was Benneit, the man who had freed him, though

he looked to have taken a vicious beating for it. Graeme beckoned him into the passageway then shouted back into the chamber, "Remember my promise, but do not take up arms against my men, or ye risk your life."

He nodded to Benneit, indicating for him to lead the way, but before they made it more than a few steps, Conn came rushing down the staircase. "My laird!"

"Speak, Conn. I chase after Merrill and Catherine. They took the tunnel. Status in the courtyard?"

"All of the warriors who attempted to fight us are dead. Some servants still circulating, some women outside the bailey. A few warriors have thrown their weapons down. Your instructions?"

Conn stared at Graeme, panting to regain control of his breathing. His brother wished to know whether they should be allowed to live. Forest green eyes popped into Graeme's mind, reminding him of Catherine's goodness, of what she had taught him, so he did not wait long to give his answer.

"Bring the servants from down here upstairs and gather everyone in the great hall. Once ye have searched the entire area, take their weapons and lead them back to our keep. I will probably be traveling in a completely different direction. My guess is that he's bringing Catherine to Beaton, the only ally he probably has at the moment."

Conn's pursed lips curved at the corners, a small sign of pleasure. "What are your plans for the rest of his clan?"

Graeme thought for a moment, then said, "I have not decided yet. Return them to our keep."

Conn nodded. "Consider it done, my laird."

He followed Benneit down to the end of the pathway and then down another staircase. At the bottom, he turned to Benneit and said, "Well done. Head back to the hall, dinnae take up a weapon, and ye may join the MacGregor clan. Your assistance will not be forgotten."

Benneit made a short bow and whispered, "Aye, my laird."

That statement told him all he needed to know about the man.

Now he just needed to find Catherine and the Merrill.

CHAPTER SEVENTEEN

CATHERINE HUGGED HER DAUGHTER TIGHT, focusing on her sweetness instead of the horror that had taken place behind them.

With Jabari by his side, Henry charged ahead as if the fire from the keep followed him. After a few hours, Catherine asked, "My lord, please, may we stop? I dinnae know if I can continue much longer. We have traveled far."

"I am not concerned with how tired you are, Catherine," Henry said. "I'd leave you behind, but I need you to convince your sire to hide us for a time."

Catherine sighed, just beginning to understand how difficult it must have been for Graeme to make it home after being held in the dungeon with so little food. She did not believe she could go on for much longer. Blisters formed inside her woolen stockings from rubbing against her boots in the uncommon terrain. She could not put Issy down, for the wee lass was too weak to travel. Her back still had not healed completely, and the pain in her ankle started again from all the running.

Her husband plunged ahead. "Catherine, if you cannot keep up, I'll leave you behind. I recall how much your sire loved my coins. Perhaps I do not need you after all."

Issy kissed her cheek, as if to say that *she* was not all right with her mother being left behind. Catherine would do anything for her daughter. Turning her head, she gave her a quick kiss. Unfortunately, taking her eyes off the terrain had been a mistake. Her foot caught in a hole and she fell, clinging to Issy so she wouldn't drop her.

Sharp pain shot up her leg from her ankle, the same one she'd hurt in her confrontation with the boar. She tried to stand on it, just then noticing that her husband had shot ahead of her.

She could see Henry giving instructions to Jabari. She rubbed her ankle, then tried to stand again without success. Jabari turned around and headed straight for them. He picked the two of them up as if they weighed no more than a feather and carried them to an outcropping of huge boulders ahead. He set Catherine and Issy down behind some rocks, underneath a ledge that would protect them if it rained, and then bowed and left to join Henry again.

"Goodbye, Catherine. Mayhap the wolves will find you." She watched her husband as he tore across the glen away from them.

Hopefully, she'd be rid of him forever.

And she prayed there were no wolves in the area.

Graeme had managed to locate two horses—one for him, and one to carry the bastard back to his keep. True, he could kill him when he found him, but his plan was to take him back and kill him on MacGregor land.

It was only right for the bastard to die on MacGregor land. He'd promised his brother and Tomag that they would be there when it happened.

Near dawn, he came upon a well-known cave not far from his land. He'd followed the trail left by one of his best men, so he was quite certain he'd find Merrill in the cave. He found a place to leave his horses a distance away, and crept up to the cave.

As soon as he was sure Merrill was inside, he pulled his claymore and stepped into the mouth of the cave. His eyes adjusted to the darkness inside, and he smiled. There, at the back of the cave, stood his prey.

Henry Merrill chuckled as soon as he saw him. Striding forward, he said, "So you've found me, MacGregor. You still hold your anger for the death of your parents. Your sire deserved it. He was a stingy man."

"Stingy? My sire was the most generous man in the Highlands."

"If he was truly generous, he would have released your mother from her marriage. She'd given him five sons. Five! He had five heirs for his land. I wanted your mother for three years. I offered him coin, begged him, but he would not release her from the marriage."

Graeme was stunned. Nothing the man could have said would have stunned him more. "Ye killed my mother, my sire, and my brother because my mother would not marry ye to give ye sons?"

"Aye," Merrill spat out. "I warned him on several occasions, but he chose to ignore me. I asked nicely at first, then I threatened. I even talked to your mother in your sire's presence, but she begged him not to accept my offer, though why he never slapped her for her insolence is beyond me."

"Because my sire was a man of honor, something ye know nothing about."

"He was warned six months before I came to your land. I told him to give her up or I'd kill her. He spoke of love. What a fool."

Graeme wished to take him by the neck and twist,

squeezing the breath out of him slowly. He could not think of a fitting fate for the bastard.

"I offered him time and coin, but he never turned her over. I should have just stolen her, but it was the principle of his audacity to me. His obstinacy had to be punished."

No wonder his sire had told Tomag to watch over them. He'd known, and this man had proven to be every bit as irrational as his sire had guessed.

"Instead, I saw the Beaton lass. Her sire refused me for a year, but the right amount of coin convinced him. What a waste of my coin. The bitch never gave me a son. You're welcome to her. She'll only give ye wenches."

"Why kill my brother? He did nothing to you." Graeme's voice had fallen to a whisper, a trick he'd learned to bring his emotions back under control.

"Your brother was just there. I killed him because I could. If I could have killed the rest of you, I would have. I hate the Scots." Merrill's fury had slowed as well. "But I could see my own warriors would balk from killing such young lads. 'Twas time to take our leave."

Merrill ran his hand through his hair, grinning. "You Scots carry this foolish sense of pride, of honor. I've had to kill too many warriors for that very word—honor. Now you think to kill me to exact revenge on me, but I am invincible. You shall fail again. Apparently, you have not noticed I have one of my best men with me." His hand motioned to the side where Jabari stood.

"Truly? I see another here, but where is your man?" Graeme took a step closer to Merrill, his hand still on the hilt of his sword.

Merrill barked, "Jabari, kill the fool. I do not feel like dirtying my hands with the blood of this scum. He is no challenge for me. He's as weak as he was seven years ago. I knew leaving him behind would pose no risk." He grinned and nodded his head to the huge man.

Jabari laughed, his white teeth shining bright even in the cave. He strode toward Merrill, rather than away, and took the villain by complete surprise when he grabbed him by the neck, lifted him off the ground, and tossed him toward Graeme.

He landed with a grunt. "What in hell are you doing, fool? I want you to kill the bastard for what he did to my wife." He stood up, cursing as he jumped back from Graeme.

But Graeme was faster. He grabbed Merrill and spun him around, throwing him to the ground and yanking his wrists behind him. "Tie him up, Jabari. We'll take him as a *guest* to my castle."

Jabari took the rope Graeme handed him and said, "With pleasure, my laird."

"My laird? You can speak? You lousy bastard! You work for MacGregor? You came onto my land under false pretenses? You'll pay for this, MacGregor."

Graeme looked at Jabari and said, "I think ye speak quite clearly. You've lost much of the sound from your homeland over the last few years."

Merrill continued to sputter as the two men tied him up. When both his hands and legs were trussed up, they brought him out of the cave. Graeme kicked Merrill with his boot, straight in his bollocks. When the lout clutched himself, groaning and shouting, Graeme said, "That's for having your wife whipped. Ye have no honor at all."

Jabari laughed when he slung Merrill over the horse. "By the way, he's just as nasty as they say. Do not feel any guilt when you kill him."

Graeme chuckled and mounted his horse. "The Mac-Gregors await your arrival." He flicked the reins of his horse and headed for home.

Finally, justice would be served.

The gates of the MacGregor castle came into view. Graeme had asked Jabari to gag Merrill because his foul mouth would not stop spouting curses. His clan deserved to witness this man's death as much as he did, else he would have taken his dirk and cut his throat.

They all needed this. He'd asked Jabari about Catherine and he'd said she was fine. He gave him instructions to get another horse and fetch her, but he didn't want her to witness what was to come. Jabari was to keep her outside the gates until the killing was done.

Her heart was too soft for what was about to happen.

Conn came out to greet him first, five MacGregor warriors with him. "Ye have the bastard and he's still alive?"

"Aye. Gather the clan in the courtyard, but first I must ask ye the status of the Merrill castle." Graeme kept his gaze focused straight ahead as they moved.

"Searched and emptied. All of the survivors here awaiting your decision. They are behind the keep."

"How many?"

"Two score of servants plus a few warriors who had thrown down their weapons and already sworn fealty to ye. They hated the Merrill. Some who tilled the land with their women and children are here. There's also a woman who claims to be his sister, but she denies him. She has a young child with her."

Once at the gates, he held up his claymore and let out the MacGregor war whoop. The time was here.

He took his time for all to gather before entering his bailey. He couldn't help but reflect on the past.

Seven years ago, his sire had sent him upstairs as soon as they heard the pounding of the horses' hooves outside their gates. He and Boyd had been playing with the dogs in the hall, while Conn and Rory had just gone to the kitchens for sweet tarts. His sire had taken Alpin with him; his mother had stayed in the hall by the hearth. Graeme had requested to stay with her, but his sire had sent him running up the stairs with Boyd.

The look on his father's face had frightened him more than anything.

He had done his best to play games with seven-year-old Boyd to distract him, but after a while, curiosity had gotten the best of him. The noise of the crowd outside had become deafening, so he'd snuck out into the passageway and clamored down the staircase, Boyd right behind him.

His mother had disappeared and the hall was empty. The quiet inside was a jarring contrast to the clamor in the courtyard, but he heard Moyra giving instructions to Conn and Rory in the kitchens. He opened the door a crack, and when he saw no one was near, he crept out onto the steps leading to the hall, his brother behind him. The first thing he noticed was the dead bodies littering the bailey, many wearing the MacGregor plaid.

His heartbeat sped up as he scanned the area, and Boyd had grabbed his arm, his fingers digging into his skin. There, in the middle of the courtyard, his sire was being held by three men. He bellowed and cursed, threatening to kill someone.

Then Graeme understood why. His mother was on her knees, sobbing, in front of a man who held a dagger at her throat. Alpin was held by another guard next to her. Boyd tugged his arm and the two huddled together as they watched the horror play out in front of them.

The cruel man sliced the knife across her throat, blood spurting everywhere, and their sire bellowed a sick sound, falling to his knees while the three men still held him.

Within moments, their sire was sobbing, something Graeme had never seen him do. He hugged Boyd, now crying, even closer as they watched.

The man, the one he now knew to be Merrill, cackled and dropped their mother's bleeding body. Then he strode forward and grabbed Alpin. Boyd's voice whispered into Graeme's ear, "Nay. Stop, please."

There was nothing they could do to stop it.

A second later, Alpin fell to the ground with a sword through his heart. His father's cries were uncontrollable by then.

This time, Merrill moved at a slower pace, giving Graeme time to think. Henry Merrill paced back and forth in front of William MacGregor, chanting and taunting him. Held back by several guards, all Graeme's father could do was sob and curse. When Merrill brought his sword up to plunge it into his belly, something snapped in Graeme, forcing him to run forward screaming, "Nay!"

His sire yelled at him, "Go back, Graeme, go back!"

But his fourteen-year-old legs propelled him forward and he jumped on the Merrill, biting him and grabbing at his arm. Henry Merrill only laughed. He stuck his sword into Graeme's father while Graeme still had his hand on his arm.

He watched from less than an arm's distance away as the life left his sire's eyes.

He also watched as Merrill twisted the sword in his sire's belly, just to make it a bit more painful.

Then Merrill turned his cruel eyes on him. "I could kill you, lad," he said, grinning—actually *grinning*, "but you are too weak. I'll leave you to tell everyone what I did. If you ever come on my land, I'll kill you the same way, in front of all. But I can tell by looking in your eyes that you are a worthless soul, a weakling. You and your pathetic little brothers will never be able to hurt me."

He tossed him backward and left, his warriors protect-ing him. As soon as he saw the back of him, Graeme fell on his sire and promised him he would seek vengeance for his death. When he finally turned around, Boyd was sitting on the ground, unmoving, an empty look in his eyes.

His brother had never said a word to anyone but him until the other day.

Well, Boyd was back, and so was he.

He'd never understood why the Merrill had murdered his family. Now he did, and Merrill would die for it.

They'd buried his family near the far curtain wall, at the far edge of the bailey. Before he would end this travesty, Graeme led his horse over to their graves and dismounted. Dropping to one knee in front of his mother's grave, he said, "I've done as I promised, Papa. Revenge is ours." He bowed his head for a moment, then stood, turning to the MacGregors behind him. He held his sword up and shouted, "Vengeance is ours!"

CHAPTER EIGHTEEN

G RAEME MOUNTED HIS HORSE AGAIN and led Starlight through the bailey, his clanmates edging both sides of the path, applauding and cheering him on. The chant, "vengeance, vengeance" followed him to the center of the courtyard. He would spill the bastard's blood in the same place where the man had killed his family.

He climbed off Starlight, tossing the reins to a stable lad, and paced a circle. He pointed to Merrill and said, "Get him off the horse. Allow him to stand in front of the Mac-Gregors, in front of his accusers."

The crowd turned wild, but he motioned them all back. He knew his men would not try to take this moment from him. Henry Merrill was his.

Once Merrill was down, his gag undone though his hands remained tied, he spat on the ground, cursing the MacGregors. Graeme gave him a moment to curse, and visions of red hair and green eyes danced through his mind.

What had she begged him to do before he'd left the dungeon? He remembered. She'd begged him to prac-tice self-control, to consider that all of Merrill's people had not hurt the MacGregors. His Catherine was a wise woman, but she did not understand what he'd seen, how he'd watched his mother die, then his brother, and his father, or how the Merrills all cheered after each death. Did they not all deserve to die for that?

Nay, only the Merrill deserved to die. Those who had chosen to try to stop them had made a poor choice. The others would be given the option to join his clan, if they chose.

As for the Merrill? He had decided Catherine was right—he could not just cut the bastard's throat. He'd fight him so the king would not question his motives. It was the fair and honest way to do it, and it would make his victory all the more satisfying. He had plenty of witnesses to vouch for him.

The only question he had not yet answered was that of Merrill's sister, the man's own flesh and blood, but Catherine's petition for mercy still rang in his head. Merrill's mother, his sister, and her child were here somewhere, though Conn had not mentioned the mother. They were not his concern at the moment. He'd decide what to do after Merrill took his last breath. Right now, he needed to focus on vengeance—for his sire, his mother, his brother, and his clan.

Graeme raised his sword, requesting silence from the crowd. "Henry Merrill, you are accused of killing William MacGregor, his dear wife Ailis, and his eldest son Alpin. For this, you have been sentenced to death."

Merrill's mouth started working on the crowd. "And who shall kill me? You? You've had seven years to kill me and done nothing. Do you fools believe he can kill me now? He will not be able to, I promise you. He's weak, and that weakness will show when he is unable to pierce my skin with that blade. Give me a sword, and I'll prove to you how weak he is. I'll kill him as I did his parents."

Graeme laughed, throwing his head back at the ridiculous suggestion. This was a man who would sooner run than lead his warriors, who would only attack enemies who had first been rendered helpless. He'd also just confessed to the MacGregor family's murder in front of countless witnesses, something that would settle things with their king, but only if he was ever questioned. "Ye think ye can fight? That ye are stronger than me?" He glanced over his shoulder at his second, standing directly behind him. "Tomag, find the bastard a sword. We shall see who is stronger."

While Tomag did as he was bid, Conn whispered in his ear, "Are ye sure about this? I'm not ready to lose another brother."

Graeme shook his head and smiled. "Do no' worry. How long have we waited for this?"

"A long time." Conn grasped his brother's shoulder. "Make me proud, Graeme."

Tomag returned with a sword in his hand.

Graeme said, "Untie his hands and give him the sword when I'm ready. Fair fight to the death after it commences."

The crowd cheered him on, and Merrill cursed them all. Graeme removed his tunic so that he wore just his plaid, the MacGregor colors. He was damn proud of those colors.

"Are ye ready, fool?" Graeme asked, getting into a fighting stance once he'd loosened up his shoulders. "Come at me. Whenever ye are ready, come at me."

Merrill swung his sword over his head with a growl, bringing it down hard on Graeme's sword. It told him just what he needed to know—there wasn't much muscle behind his thrust. Still, he decided to let the bastard swing for a while before he delivered the killing blow.

The fool sliced his sword from the side, aiming for his belly, but Graeme blocked him easily. They parried for a while, sword against sword, the crowd chanting.

This battle with his enemy gave Graeme a kind of focus he'd never experienced before. Everything moved to the center of his field of vision. He could see the man was weakening, so he teased him with his next thrust, catching him from the side, drawing blood with a small cut across his chest, not deep at all.

The shock on Merrill's face gave him immense satisfaction. His opponent stepped back to assess the damage.

While he paused, Graeme's sire's face popped into his mind, then his mother's, her smile as loving as it had always been when he was young. How he'd loved his parents. He wiped the sweat from his face as he gathered all his strength inward—a lesson his sire had taught him so long ago. "Power comes from your inner strength, lad, not from the size of your muscles."

Even so, he'd spent seven years building his muscles and his skills for this moment. The Merrill would not live much longer. But he wouldn't go down easily either. While weak, he did have some battle skills. That fact would only sweeten the MacGregor win.

Once the Merrill regained control after his injury, the blood still trickling down his side, he started taunting Graeme, similar to how he'd done it seven years ago. "You are still weak, MacGregor, just as your sire was. He was no challenge for me, and neither are you."

The crowd went wild, thumping their feet at his enemy's words. This time, instead of being on the defense, Graeme would take the offense.

Sweat covered him as the morning sun beat down on them. He flexed his muscles, then came at the bastard with a power he had not known was inside him. He swung and almost knocked Merrill off his feet.

"That was a good swing for a weakling." Merrill swung at him from the right, a direct blow he easily blocked, but he was surprised to see his enemy switch directions at the last moment and come at him from the other side.

Graeme adjusted and blocked Merrill's next blow, steel on steel ringing out louder than the cries of the crowd. They circled each other again. Alpin's face surfaced in his mind. *Do this, Graeme.*

Graeme came at him hard, swinging his claymore in a wide arc, intent on knocking his weapon out of his hand, but he'd anticipated the man's next move wrong, and Merrill swung an underhanded blow at him, cutting the skin under his arm open, spilling blood down his side in a river.

Graeme dropped to one knee to keep from falling over, but such a blow would not stop him. He mustered the power to stand up again. Then one sound rang out above the racket of the crowd.

"Nay, Graeme!"

Catherine.

Catherine and Issy had stayed in the very spot where Jabari had left them. Catherine had said a silent prayer that Graeme would find them, though the strange man had hidden them so well that she had no idea how anyone could find them. At first, she kept quiet, listening for Henry or any creatures that could be out there, but the woods were quiet except for the hoot of an owl or the soft sounds of a breeze stirring the leaves of the trees. After a while, she did the only thing she could do. She lay down on her side, cuddling Issy to her, and closed her eyes, hoping the wild animals would leave them be.

Issy had patted her cheek and said, "I love you, Mama." Her eyes had closed, and she'd fallen fast asleep before Catherine could profess her love for her sweet daughter.

Some time later, a voice spoke her name, and she sat straight up, doing her best to protect her daughter. Her mind was fuzzy, but she glanced around the rock to see Jabari standing there, holding his hand out to her. "Come, my lady. I'll take you to the MacGregor."

The sun was up, but not far. Before Catherine could wrap her arms tighter around her daughter, Issy stepped away from her and straight into Jabari's arms. "Look, Mama. He talks."

Catherine looked at the man in confusion. "Nay, Jabari. I'll not go back to Henry. I'll wait for someone else to come." Tears filled her eyes as she thought of her husband's brutality. "No more. We'll not go with ye."

Issy asked, "Why, Mama? I like Jabari."

Jabari laughed and explained, "I do not work for your husband. I belong to the MacGregor clan, and Graeme sent me to retrieve you. I'll take you to his castle."

"What? But ye were with my husband. Ye were my guard. How can that be?"

"Graeme sent me to watch over you after he escaped. He hired me to protect you from your daft husband. Merrill hired me as a guard because the MacGregor had a man on the inside act as an intermediary between us. It was easy because your husband was desperate, and he liked the idea of a guard who couldn't speak. He had already lost many men." He held his hand out to her and said, "I promised to hide ye well while I led Merrill straight into the MacGregor's arms. And I had an inner peace that told me you would stay where I left you."

"But what if we *had* left?"

He winked at her. "I have a special talent for finding

people I'm assigned to. I would have found you. Come, I'll take you to Graeme."

"My husband?"

"I doubt your husband is still alive. The MacGregor and I took him to his castle. They were about to do battle when I left."

"Battle?"

"Aye. The MacGregor has so much honor that even he could not kill his worst enemy in cold blood. He preferred to kill him in battle, so when I left they were about to fight in the courtyard. I'm sure it is done now."

She placed her hand in Jabari's and he helped her down from the rocks, though her ankle still pained her. He'd brought a horse for them, and he helped her and Issy get settled before he mounted his own animal. Less than an hour later, they were outside the curtain wall. The air rang with the shouts of an enraged crowd, wild with the fervor of the battle. The gates opened for them, and they quickly rode across the bridge.

Jabari led them to the stables and helped her down. "My lady, the MacGregor did not want you to witness the fight. Why not wait under the nice shade tree in the corner? I'll take Issy over there so she'll not see anything."

She was at just a high enough vantage point to see the chaos unfold beneath her. Graeme fought her husband in the middle of the courtyard, and rows and rows of warriors watched the swordfight, cheering for the MacGregor. She turned and handed her daughter to the gentle giant. "Take her, please, Jabari. I must stay." Once they headed off to the shade tree, she turned back toward the courtyard.

When the combatants finally appeared in her line of vision, she watched as husband sliced Graeme's side, and blood poured out of his body, dripping all over the ground.

She screamed, "Nay, Graeme!" She would not, could

not watch the man she loved die in front of her. Bolting toward the middle of the melee, she was stopped short when pain shot up her leg from the pressure of running. No matter—she'd have to ignore her pain.

She shoved at all the warriors between her and her love, pushing and limping her way through the crowd. She had to get to the front.

If she had to, she'd stick a dagger in Henry Merrill's black heart herself.

CHAPTER NINETEEN

O UT OF THE CORNER OF his eye, he saw Catherine in the distance, just the fuel he needed. He ignored the slight pain in his side.

"Weak!" Merrill taunted. "Just as I said before." He swung his sword again at Graeme, aiming for him when he had his head turned, running straight at him. "You worthless soul. You deserve to die! Once I'm finished with you, I'll kill my whore wife, too."

The world slowed in front of Graeme. A daft man ran straight at him, his sword aimed at Graeme's heart. His mother's voice called to him, "Graeme, be strong. You are such a good lad." Catherine's sweet smile appeared in front of him, her hand reaching out to cup his cheek. Then he saw all of his brothers, living and dead, standing together in a cluster. "End this, Graeme. Please?" Boyd asked.

He had no idea what was reality and what was his memory, for his every bit of consciousness was focused on the man coming straight at him. He blinked once and then slashed his sword from the side with both hands, striking at Merrill's hands. The villain's blade went flying into the air and his eyes widened with sudden fear at this change in events. Then the point of Graeme's sword drove straight into Merrill's belly.

Graeme gripped his sword with both hands and with a grunt, bellowed above the crowd, "This is for my sire, William MacGregor." He took a step closer to his enemy and twisted the sword in his belly, the lout's eyes now rolling back as he grappled to remove the sword from his innards. "This is for Ailis MacGregor." He twisted his sword again. "And this is for my brother, Alpin."

He grabbed Merrill's shoulder to give him leverage to yank the blade out. The mob erupted into cheering and chanting, "MacGregor, MacGregor, MacGregor."

Then he thrust the sword straight into the bastard's heart and said, "And this is for Catherine."

His hands fell away from his blade, and he watched his enemy go down, dead at last. He heard Rory and Conn shouting, and Tomag had already pushed through the crowd and was pounding his back, shoving something in his hands. Graeme looked down to see a rock with carvings on it. He peered up at Tomag, confused.

"Your sire's good luck charm. It belongs to ye, you've earned it." Too much in shock from all that had happened, he tucked it away and searched the crowd for someone. He was pleased his people were celebrating his victory, but they weren't what he needed.

He needed Catherine. He needed to see that she would not reject him for killing her husband. Turning toward her screams, he pushed through the crowd until he found her, tears streaming down her face. She leaped into his arms and he said a quick prayer of thanks to the Lord that she had accepted what he had to do.

She cupped his face and said, "I love you."

"I love you, too."

"Issy?" he whispered. "Where is your daughter? She was

with you, was she not?"

Catherine's fingers moved to his lips to silence him. "She is with Jabari. She loves him."

He sighed with relief. "Jabari will protect her."

A silence fell around them, but Graeme would not, could not, let go of Catherine. Holding her tight, he pivoted to see what had quieted the crowd so suddenly.

Boyd. His younger brother, who was just beginning to come out of his shell, moved down the steps. It was a slow but deliberate walk, and he did it with his head held high. Catherine turned her head to watch him with the rest of the MacGregors, resting her face against Graeme's chest, tears still falling down her cheeks, and he set his hand on her neck, caressing her just at the base of her hairline.

Boyd did not even look at them, instead moving to the center of the courtyard to the body of Henry Merrill. Graeme thought to intercept him, but Tomag caught his gaze and shook his head, indicating they needed to give Boyd this moment. The silence held for a moment, everyone's gaze pinned on the lad who had still not said a word to anyone outside the keep. Once he reached the Merrill, he paused, glancing at the body surrounded by a pool of blood. Then he bent over and pulled Graeme's sword out of the bastard's heart.

The mob erupted in cheers, chanting Boyd's name. Graeme could tell he struggled to carry the heavy sword, but he lifted it into the air and walked away from all of them. The throng parted as Boyd made his path away from the keep. Graeme had no idea where he was headed until he made it down past the stables and turned to the left.

He was heading for their family's graves. Graeme followed behind him, unsure of what he might do, taking Catherine with him. The others came, too. When they arrived at the gravesite, everyone hushed again out of respect.

Boyd knelt in front of their mother's grave—their sire to the left and Alpin to the right.

Rory pushed his way through the crowd and knelt on Boyd's right side, settling his hand on the hilt of the sword with his brother's as if he knew exactly what his brother planned. The two set the sword crosswise so it touched all three graves, and bowed their heads for a moment of silence before they stood.

Boyd said, "For ye, Mama, and for ye, Papa, and ye, Alpin."

Graeme and Conn joined their brothers, clasping their shoulders. Conn yelled, "For the MacGregors, all of us."

The group erupted in cheers again, and Boyd turned to smile at Graeme. "Done," he said. "'Tis finally done, Graeme."

The crowd followed the brothers as they moved up the path and across the courtyard, almost crushing them, but Graeme protected Catherine and found his way up to the steps heading into the great hall.

With his arm around her, he stood at the top of the steps and held his hand up, asking the crowd for silence.

When they finally quieted, he looked at Conn and said, "Bring the prisoners into the courtyard."

Graeme felt Catherine's body tense in his arms, but he just squeezed her close and looked at his brothers.

He knew what he had to do.

It was just and right, though he knew many would disagree with him.

As soon as Catherine heard the word "prisoners," her knees buckled, but she clung to Graeme, saying another prayer in her heart that he would do the right thing. That he'd brought them here was a good sign. Would he offer them escape or a place in the clan? Or did he intend to have the remaining warriors put to death? To slay Margaret and the others in front of his clan? From their screams and cries, the men were still thirsty for vengeance.

Tomag and Conn led the first group that had been held behind the keep into the middle of the courtyard, pushing the throng of warriors back to protect the men, women, and children marching through their ranks.

Catherine dared to peek out at the group, surprised at the number of people, most of them servants she recognized. The fear in their eyes ripped her insides out. Her gaze found Dolag, who looked as if she would faint. She tore her gaze away from her beloved maid and found her husband's cook, two maids who had helped her often, the maids' daughters, and finally Benneit. She'd worried what would become of him after Henry discovered his role in Graeme's escape. He looked like he'd been badly beaten, but he was *alive*. They all faced Graeme, along with many others, waiting to hear their fate.

Graeme held his hand up to silence the crowd. "Are there more, Conn?"

"Aye. Two more groups."

Graeme said, "Bring out the warriors."

Moments later, a small group of warriors emerged, along with some families, clinging to each other.

Graeme glanced at the families. "Ye work the land?"

The men in the crowd nodded, one offering, "We'd be honored to work your land, my laird."

Graeme looked to Conn again. "And the last group? Bring them here."

Conn nodded and left to do what he was bid. Catherine dared to peek out at the large group in front of her, many people she'd never known although she was their mistress. Why? Because her husband had kept her almost as a prisoner would be kept, confined to their chamber above stairs. She did not regret his death.

When the last group entered the courtyard, Catherine could not help but squeeze Graeme tighter. It consisted of two people.

Margaret and Wesley. As soon as they stood in front of her, Wesley said, "Greetings, Aunt Catherine. Where is Isbeil?" He grinned at her, a toothless grin because he'd lost his two front teeth.

Graeme asked, "Ye are sister to the Merrill?"

Margaret met his gaze without flinching and replied, "Yes. I am his sister, but I renounce his ways. He was a cruel man, especially to his wife." She nodded toward Catherine.

The crowd of MacGregors erupted at the declaration that she was his sister, some shouting for their deaths, some shouting to save them. Catherine did all she could to stay on her feet, but the exhaustion of the past fortnight was finally taking its toll. She still had her head resting on Graeme's bare chest, comforted by his touch in this chaos unfolding around her. Her arms were wrapped tight around his waist, and when her anxiety became too much for her, she chose to bury her face against his chest and not look at anyone. What would he decide about Margaret and dear Wes?

Graeme whispered in her ear. "Do ye trust me, Catherine?"

She did not answer right away. She could not.

Did she trust him?

He had taken the life of her husband and, in so doing, put an end to her life of beatings, humiliation, and hatred. It was the greatest gift she could ever imagine. She'd never again have to worry about how Henry would treat their daughter when she grew up.

He had taught her that a man's touch could be tender and loving; he'd caressed her as though she was a delicate flower but allowed her to be herself, listened to her like no one else ever had. And he had shown her a fleeting glimpse of what it would be like to love a good man.

Did she trust him? Or did she need to drop to her knees and beg him to forgive Margaret and Wesley for being related to a bad man? He'd promised to save the other women and children, but what about the rest? The men who'd toiled in her husband's fields? The warriors who'd chosen to lay down their swords rather than fight for the Merrill?

She stood back and gazed into his eyes, those beautiful blue eyes that looked at her as though she was the most special being in all the land, and said, "Aye. I trust ye, Graeme, with all my heart."

He kissed her forehead and turned to the crowd, taking his brother Conn's sword and holding it above his head as the throng cheered. He waited for silence before his pronouncement, though the sobbing of women could be heard through the quiet.

When he held the sword at its highest point, he said, "The killing stops here. You may choose to join the MacGregor clan if ye are willing to swear fealty to me, or we shall escort ye to a land far away. Ye have a sennight to decide." The crowd cheered his decision. Even the dissenters who'd called for Henry's family to be put to death were caught up in the joy of the moment, or at least silenced by the others' cheers, and the prisoners hugged each other in relief. Tears ran down Margaret's cheek as she kissed wee Wesley. Graeme's brothers practically beamed with pride—Boyd smiled at him and Conn clapped him on the back.

Catherine jumped up and down, still clinging to him, tears of joy falling down her face. She kissed his cheek as he beckoned for silence again.

"There is one last thing I must do." He leaned over and whispered to Tomag while the group quieted again.

Catherine had no idea what was about to happen, but she would give this man whom she adored so much whatever he wished. She trusted him.

Once silence reigned again, Graeme dropped to one knee in front of Catherine. Her knees began shaking as soon as he brought his gaze to hers, smiling that beautiful smile she so loved. What was he about? Was this as he'd promised in the dungeon? She fingered the beautiful necklace he'd given her in troth.

He took her hand in his and said in a voice loud enough for all to hear, "Catherine, ye have shown me a life I never knew existed, one of love, of laughter, of sharing, of giving." He bowed his head for a moment as if he needed to gather himself, but when he lifted his gaze back to hers, she noticed the misting in his eyes.

"I love ye with all my heart, and while others would advise me to wait, I find I cannae. I ask ye to marry me, to be my wife, to always walk beside me, to bear my children, and to continue to give me the unconditional love and trust ye have already gifted me with on this day. I vow to love ye and walk beside ye forever, to protect ye and honor ye as ye so deserve."

Catherine giggled, unable to believe all that had just transpired, but nothing could stop her from pledging to spend her life loving this man. She shrieked, "Aye!" and threw herself at him, wrapping her arms around his neck and almost toppling him over, much to the delight of their audience. When he stood, Catherine in his arms, he glanced out over the crowd and nodded his head to someone in the distance.

While they waited, he cupped her face and said, "I love you."

"Graeme, I promise to love ye forever."

The crowd parted again, all turning around to see whom Graeme had summoned. Four people came forward with Tomag, though they were kept hidden from Catherine.

CHAPTER TWENTY

GRAEME HAD TOLD TOMAG TO fetch some very special people after he removed the body from the courtyard. Graeme took Catherine's hand and turned tc watch Jabari come their way. He carried a most special gift—a wee lassie whom Graeme was most anxious to meet. In fact, as the pair moved closer to the stairs, something lodged in his throat, though he knew not what.

In Jabari's hands was a miniature Catherine, a wee doll, a beautiful child. He glanced at Catherine, her face lit up with radiance and pride at the sight of her daughter.

Issy enchanted the crowd as Jabari carried her through them, now up on his big dark shoulders, her tiny hands wrapped under his chin. She yelled, "Greetings, Mama," and waved her tiny hand at her mother. "I love Jabari. He is fun to play with." Jabari's smile was wider than Graeme had ever seen it. Clearly, he was as enchanted with Isbeil as she was with him.

Catherine giggled at her daughter's playfulness, squeezing Graeme's hand. When Issy drew close, she lifted her hand to someone in the courtyard. "Greetings, Dolag and Aunt Margaret, I missed all of ye, but I'm pleased to see ye again, especially Wesley."

Then the lassie waved her tiny hand to everyone in the crowd, giggling, and before long, the crowd laughed with her. "Mama, I love the sun. Do ye not all love the sun? 'Tis so warm today. Mama, Jabari played a game with me where I would hide and he had to find me. He could not find me." Then she bent her head forward to see if she could look into Jabari's eyes, her face almost upside-down in front of him. "Is that not right, Jabari? I am a very good hider. Ye could not find me."

Jabari erupted into the loudest laugh Graeme had ever heard from anyone, his entire body shaking from the joy of the wee one on his shoulders. Echoes of laughter spread through the crowd of MacGregors, something Graeme had not heard in years. When Jabari finally made it to the stairs, he stopped halfway up so that Issy was face-to-face with Graeme. "Greetings, my lord," she said. "My name is Isbeil. Greetings, Mama. See how big I am? I'm bigger than ye."

Graeme laughed, soaking in the joy he saw in his loved ones' faces. But he had something important to do.

"Greetings to ye, Isbeil." Silence settled again. "I have something important to ask you. Will ye listen for a moment?"

She nodded. "Aye." Her hands patted the top of Jabari's shaved bald head.

"Issy, I have asked Mama to marry me, and she has agreed, but I would like your permission to marry your mama."

A puzzled expression stole across Issy's face, and she looked to her mother for guidance. All of a sudden, Graeme realized the problem. Did she understand that her sire was dead?

Catherine held her arms out to her daughter, and Jabari bent down so Graeme could lift Issy from his shoulders and into Catherine's arms. "Issy, Papa has gone away and he'll never come back. I would like to marry Graeme MacGregor so we can live here with him. What do ye think?"

The lassie's fingers came to her lips, and she pivoted her head around to look at all the happy people surrounding her. Graeme noticed Boyd and Rory nodding to her in encouragement, even Dolag and others in the crowd she did not know were smiling at her.

She turned back to Graeme and then put her wee hand on her mother's cheek. "Aye, Mama. Do ye know why?"

"Why?"

"Because Graeme smiles, and Papa never did. No one at home smiled." She turned around at the hush that had settled over everyone. "Even Dolag smiles here. May we stay, my lord?"

Graeme nodded and kissed her headful of red curls. "Nothing would please me more."

"May I play outside here?"

"Aye, ye may play outside whenever…" He cast a glance at Catherine, changing what he was about to say. "Whenever your mother says ye may."

Everyone laughed, Jabari stepped back and moved away, giving room for a third person to approach the new family—Father MacLean.

Graeme asked, "Father, would ye do me the honor of marrying me to this lovely lady, Catherine?"

"Ye wish to marry now, both of ye?"

Catherine nodded, then walked over and handed Issy to Dolag before returning to them.

Graeme held his hand up to the priest. "Wait, please. There is one more person we need." He motioned to Tomag, who stood off to the side. Once Tomag had informed him about how unhappy Catherine's sister was at their home, he'd sent a guard to the Beaton to collect her.

Tomag came forward, leading someone behind him. When he reached the steps, he stepped aside and Catherine screamed. There stood her sister, Anna, who ran up the steps to hug her.

"Anna? How did ye get here?"

Her sister, whom she adored, pointed to Graeme and said, "He brought me here, thankfully, and ye are blessed, Catherine." She kissed her sister's cheek. "Marry him, ye will be so happy together."

Graeme motioned to Father MacLean, who joined them, motioning for Anna to stand by Catherine, and for Conn, Boyd, and Rory to stand beside their brother. Dolag handed Issy back to Catherine.

Father MacLean placed Catherine's hand in Graeme's and wrapped a length of the blue and red MacGregor plaid over their entwined hands. He made the sign of the cross, then began.

"This is a most unusual day, and I find myself at a loss for words, so these will not be my usual wedding verses. I received the request to come to the MacGregor land a few days ago, and I dreaded the journey. I have felt the pain of your clan for many years, Graeme MacGregor. I feared I had been called to place a blessing upon a bloodbath, though no one could blame ye for wanting revenge.

"I prayed for strength to do what the Lord needed me to do when I arrived, prayed that some special light could come here to help this clan put their tragic past behind them."

Graeme heard several indrawn and hitching breaths from the crowd. Had he done the right thing by accepting Catherine's people into his clan, forgiving them, not holding them accountable for the evils of a few? Or did his clan believe he had wronged them? Time would tell, but what did Father MacLean believe?

Father MacLean continued. "I could not be more pleased by what has taken place here. Aye, vengeance is yours against an evil, blighted soul, as it should be. But ye have opened your heart to a lovely woman, and opened your clan to some good people. I believe they will serve ye well, my laird, and bring love and happiness back to ye all. I offer my blessing and the Lord's blessing to this union, this light that has been brought to a most deserving clan. May ye put the hatred behind ye. I pray that the Lord will bless ye and your clan with many bairns, much happiness, and strength and wisdom to guide ye on your way."

He took out a linen square and dabbed at his eyes before continuing. "Catherine, do ye love this man and take him to be your husband?" Catherine glanced up at Graeme and said, "Aye."

"And Graeme MacGregor, do ye love this woman and take her to be your wife?"

"Aye, I do, with pleasure." He laughed and so did Catherine.

Father MacLean paused, then glanced over his shoulder. "And…" he leaned over to whisper something to Catherine, who whispered her response. "And Isbeil, do ye accept Graeme MacGregor and his clan as your family?"

Issy cried, "Aye," waving her wee hands in the air.

"Graeme MacGregor, kiss your new wife."

Graeme leaned down and kissed his wife, doing his best to let her know how much she meant to him. When he ended the kiss, the love in her eyes spoke to him like nothing else ever had. She wrapped her hand around his neck and gazed into his eyes. "I love you. Forgive me for ever doubting ye. I thank ye from the bottom of my heart."

Before long, his soft-hearted wife sobbed and laughed at the same time, surrounded by all the special people in their lives.

But she never let go of him, and he was quite happy about that.

Because he knew, without a doubt, that he'd never, ever, let her go.

CHAPTER TWENTY-ONE

Six months later…

CATHERINE AND GRAEME STOOD NEAR the stables, arm in arm, Graeme with his arm wrapped around Catherine in a warm embrace against the early winter winds of the Highlands.

"Must ye go, Jabari?" Catherine asked, glancing off to the side at Issy, presently running circles around the three of them, kicking the leaves around as she shuffled her feet in the grass.

"Aye, my lady, I must. I miss the heat of my lands. It is time for me to return to my family, find myself a good woman like Graeme has, bring some wee ones into the world."

"Why did ye ever leave?" Catherine asked.

He packed a few things into his saddle bag. "Something happened to me in my land, so different from here, lush with overgrowth. We have bananas and fruits you have never seen. I set off to retrieve some sweet fruit for a girl I admired, and I found myself hit over the head and tied up. I was thrown on a ship and sent across the waters to England. The men of the ship wished to sell me off as if

I were nothing more than a bolt of cloth. I was fortu-
nate. Graeme here bought me, but he did not treat me as
though he owned me."

"Why were ye there, Graeme?" Catherine looked up at
her husband, a man she loved more every day.

"We were in London trying to convince the king of
the Merrill's guilt. We often walked the streets searching
for goods to bring home—cloth, weaponry, leather goods.
Down a side street, we came upon this group of unsavory
Englishmen selling men they had stolen from a distant
land. I know not why, but one look at Jabari, his size,
the expression in his eyes, told me he was a good man. I
bought him to be a warrior, not to own. I'd hoped he'd
agree to fight with us against the bastard for coin."

"We'd heard it many times in my land," Jabari said, staring into the mountains. "Centuries ago, many ships stole
our people to sell in other lands, but they'd said it had
stopped. This group of men? No one knows what drove
them. They did their best to hide us once they reached
London, so I knew it was not common practice to treat
my people like animals, but when you are tied up, you
have no choice. I wished to beat Graeme to a pulp, but,"
he grasped Graeme's shoulder, "he earned my loyalty and
my respect. He had the fire in him for vengeance, so I
agreed to help him." He glanced at the gray sky above,
clouds rolling by. "I've been in the Highlands for many
winters now, and while I may miss the view of your
mountains and your cool summer breezes, I will not miss
your winters. I leave before another is thrust upon me."

"We shall miss ye terribly." Catherine hugged Graeme,
resting her head on him.

"Aye, well, you must take care of that laddie you have
in your belly," he pointed to her obviously rounded abdo-
men. "Someday maybe I'll have a lad of my own." He

reached over to touch her red curls. "When I tell my family of the red-gold, they'll never believe me."

Graeme grasped his shoulder, "Many thanks for all you've done for us, Jabari."

"You are welcome. And I thank you for the gift of gold coins to buy my passage home."

"Need I remind ye who hid the gold coins and brought them to me after I married my beautiful wife?"

"I knew the Merrill would not have any use for those coins." He sighed as he glanced from Graeme to Catherine, and finally to sweet Issy. "Truth is, you do not need me anymore. Your clan is strong, and your wife is not the only one expecting a babe soon. May the MacGregors forever flourish."

Issy paused in her jumping. "But I need ye, Jabari. How will I ever pick the best apples from the trees again?"

Jabari reached down and swung the lass up into the trees with a whoosh and a rush of giggles from her before he set her down again.

"Ye were correct about the sunshine, Jabari. I had never thought of the harm of leaving someone in a cellar." Catherine laughed at her daughter's joy. It was wonderful to see her healthy and strong.

"It was out of your control, my lady. I'm glad I could be of assistance."

"You were, Jabari. For some reason, I trusted ye from the first moment we met. It was as if ye had been sent to help me. Many, many thanks to ye, and I wish you a wonderful and safe journey." She kissed his cheek and hugged him.

He mounted his horse and left with a wave.

Catherine shouted after him, "Come back and visit someday?"

He laughed, "Do not worry. I'll be watching."

EPILOGUE

Forty years later, somewhere in heaven

CATHERINE LEANED HER HEAD ON her husband's shoulder, sighing so deeply that he chuckled. In this place they were young again, and each reveled in the limitations that had been lifted from their aging bodies.

"You like me young and handsome again, sweetness?" He glanced down at her, the corners of his mouth curving up.

"You were always the most handsome of all to me, Graeme."

They cuddled a little closer, both of them transfixed by the large clear screen that took up the entire wall in front of them. They had been watching their family for some time now. A light knock landed on the door, and Evangeline strolled into the room. She nodded to them and sat in the chair beside the couch they were sitting on together.

The three of them watched the screen. There it was— the Highlands in all its beauty, the peaks in the distance now snow-covered while the pines whispered in the wind. It was a beautiful winter day back home, and they watched as Boyd moved toward the new keep they'd built ten years ago because their family had grown so large. He stepped inside the door and moved down a few steps to the center of the MacGregor great hall, roaring like a monster and shaking the snow off his shoulders, making a point to shake it over a gaggle of children laughing and giggling in front of him.

"You did a fine job with Boyd," Evangeline said. "I was very worried about him, but with the love from both of you, he turned into a fine husband and father."

Catherine glanced up at her husband's smiling face. "We did, didn't we?"

Evangeline crossed her arms as she watched the others greet Boyd in the hall. "Issy, too. She grew into a lovely young lass. Graeme, I must commend you for accepting her as your own in your heart. And what a fine family you two had together, four lads and two more lassies."

Graeme leaned down to kiss Catherine's forehead.

"I was not surprised you chose to leave at the same time. True, it was difficult for your children, but I think it was no surprise to the rest of your clan. The fever came and took you both, and you handled it as well as you could."

Graeme looked at Catherine. "No tears, wife, after leaving our bairns and grandbairns?"

Evangeline laughed. "You know there's no crying here, Graeme."

"Why is that?" He glanced over at their guide.

"There is no pain in heaven, and crying would be caused by an ache inside. We do not allow that. You have both suffered enough, don't you agree? This is the place of happiness and celebration."

Catherine whispered as she squeezed her husband's hand. "It only made us stronger." She fingered the necklace that Graeme had given her, somehow still around her neck.

Graeme added, "It made us appreciate our time together afterward, each newborn, each smile."

"True, and you left behind many strong MacGregors to carry your legacy into the future, just as we asked you to do." Evangeline got up from her chair and moved to stand in front of them. "I must say you did a wonderful job for your first challenge, even better than expected. Do you wish to know where we will send you next?"

"Next?" Graeme glanced at Catherine. "Already?"

"We'll give you a week to enjoy yourselves, visit with your family who passed before you, relax a bit. But then we will send you on to your next life."

"Scotland, again?" Graeme asked.

Catherine said, "Please, no war this time." She rubbed her forehead, the vague memory of battles and wars from previous lives breaking into her thoughts.

"That would be most difficult," Evangeline said softly. She reached out and squeezed Catherine's hand before pulling back. "You see, this may surprise you, but you were brought here, Catherine, because handling the difficulties of war is one of your strong suits. Graeme is one of our finest warriors and leaders. We angels work to bring about a future day of peace for all of humanity, but we're still a long way from achieving our goal, and it is human nature to have conflict and challenges."

Graeme gave Evangeline a puzzled look. "So do we move forward with each life? We will be born after the 1500s?"

Evangeline shook her head. "Not necessarily. Catherine's previous life was in the Americas in the 1800s. We look at where we think you can bring about the best change. Heaven is not as linear as it appears to you on earth. If we decide to alter history, we can do that. It takes powerful spirits to inspire such change, something you may not be ready for yet. Maybe someday in a different life."

Catherine glanced up at Graeme. "But he will find me, right? You will lead us to each other, correct?"

She nodded. "Your guiding and guardian angels will lead you to each other, but it is up to *you*, your human spirits, whether or not you will listen to your intuition. You also will carry your tokens with you." She pointed toward Catherine's necklace and then nodded to Graeme, who pulled out the lucky charm given to him by his sire. "Both of those will travel with you. We use the tokens to trigger memories."

"So we will be able to recall our time together?"

Evangeline smiled. "No, you will not. I'm afraid it would cause a stir among humans. We never plant the solid memory of heaven, just fleeting glimpses. These tokens will help pull you toward your soulmate."

Graeme kissed her cheek. "I will find you again, I promise."

"And Graeme?" Evangeline added. "This time Catherine will be the one who needs your help to reach the light."

Graeme picked her up and settled her on his lap, wrapping his arms around her. "I look forward to the challenge."

THE END

NOVELS BY

KEIRA MONTCLAIR

ASHLYN-BOOK FIVE
MOLLY-BOOK SIX
JAMIE AND GRACIE- BOOK SEVEN
SORCHA-BOOK EIGHT
KYLA-BOOK NINE
BETHIA-BOOK TEN
LOKI'S CHRISTMAS STORY-BOOK ELEVEN

–

THE BAND OF COUSINS
HIGHLAND VENGEANCE
HIGHLAND ABDUCTION
HIGHLAND RETRIBUTION
HIGHLAND LIES
HIGHLAND FORTITUDE
HIGHLAND RESILIENCE
HIGHLAND DEVOTION
HIGHLAND BRAWN
HIGHLAND YULETIDE MAGIC

–

HIGHLAND SWORDS
THE SCOT'S BETRAYAL

–

THE SOULMATE CHRONICLES
#1 TRUSTING A HIGHLANDER
#2 TRUSTING A SCOT

–

STAND–ALONE BOOKS
THE BANISHED HIGHLANDER
REFORMING THE DUKE
WOLF AND THE WILD SCOTS
*FALLING FOR THE CHIEFTAIN-3RD IN A COL-
LABORATIVE TRILOGY*

–

THE SUMMERHILL SERIES–
CONTEMPORARY ROMANCE
#1-ONE SUMMERHILL DAY
#2-A FRESH START FOR TWO
#3-THREE REASONS TO LOVE

DEAR READER,

Thank you for reading Graeme and Catherine's story. I absolutely loved telling their story. I do plan to write another story about our soulmates, Graeme and Catherine, but I have no immediate date for their next journey. When their story calls to me again (and I have no idea where they will travel for their next journey), I will write it.

As discussed in the prologue, Graeme and Catherine each have their own guardian angel. Did you guess who belonged to whom?

Tomag was Graeme's guardian angel, and Catherine's guardian? Why, Jabari, of course!

Jabari was absolutely correct (he's an angel, so of course he was right) that Issy's only problem was from being holed up in a cellar for most of her young life. She had a severe Vitamin D deficiency. Medieval times were full of vitamin deficiencies because they did not know much about nutrition, but what most of them did have was sunlight. The rays of the sun on our skin are our greatest source of Vitamin D. Boyd also suffered from the same ailment, and once he began to move outside again, his strength returned.

Today, many suffer from a Vitamin D deficiency because we are so good about using our sunscreen. If this is you, make sure you take a vitamin D supplement. I do, because I had a deficiency myself. (The RN part of me is done teaching. Sorry!)

Africans were frequently sold in the 11th century and earlier, but then that horrid practice slowed down until the 17th century and later. Since the story is completely fictional, I didn't think it a stretch to imagine there were still some fools out there who would attempt the practice in the 15th century.

They sold women; they sold men.

Medieval times were hard.

What's next on my agenda?

My next novel will be Sorcha's story in The Highland Clan. I have it already plotted, and I think you will love it.

TO SIGN UP FOR MY NEWSLETTER:
www.keiramontclair.com
MY FACEBOOK PAGE:
www.facebook.com/KeiraMontclair/
MY PINTEREST PAGE:
www.pinterest.com/KeiraMontclair/

If you enjoy my writing, the best thing you can do to support me is to write a review on any of my novels at retail sites or Goodreads, and tell your friends about my books.

Happy reading!

Keira Montclair

ABOUT THE AUTHOR

KEIRA MONTCLAIR IS THE PEN name of an author who lives in Florida with her husband. She loves to write fast-paced, emotional romance, especially with children as secondary characters in her stories.

She has worked as a registered nurse in pediatrics and recovery room nursing. Teaching is another of her loves, and she has taught both high school mathematics and practical nursing.

Now she loves to spend her time writing, but there isn't enough time to write everything she wants! Her Highlander Clan Grant series, comprising of eight standalone novels, is a reader favorite. Her third series, The Highland Clan, set twenty years after the Clan Grant series, focuses on the Grant/Ramsay descendants. She also has a contemporary series set in The Finger Lakes of Western New York.